SIR THOMAS
and the
Golden
DRAGON

BRANDON FARLOW

PAGE PUBLISHING
Conneaut Lake, PA

First originally published by Page Publishing 2024

ISBN 979-8-89315-962-2 (pbk)
ISBN 979-8-89315-980-6 (digital)

Printed in the United States of America

CHAPTER

1

THOMAS MELVIEW WAS a boy of eight years old when he first heard about the golden dragon.

"I'll tell you a tale, my son, of a great golden dragon that is so rare that one scale on its mighty hide can make a man rich for all his life," Thomas's father told Thomas. "I was ten years old when my father told me the tale, and for many years, I sought out the legendary dragon. When King Midorian, of the first kingdom of Tronsel, was but a young boy, he traveled far and wide to find a place he belonged. He could not do hard labor, for he was too frail and meek. He could not be a scholar, as he was too lazy to learn the words of both magic and gods alike. And he could not be a servant in the quarters of a home as he was sickened by almost everything. How, then, might you ask, did such a man become king of our land? Well, it was because he met the golden dragon, and according to him, it gifted him a golden scale which he used to become the richest in the whole land. With his wealth, he assisted everyone in the kingdom in any way he could. Thus, over time, he was claimed as king. When he became king, he visited the place where he found the golden dragon, and upon a tree was a message that said, 'Your Majesty, our meeting was fated to be so, and I will return one day. And on that day, I will come and bless a new simple man, and he too shall become king and rule in your place.' Signed, Narvaria the Golden Dragon."

"Father, this is nothing more than a fable," Thomas said. "Besides, even if it were true, where's the dragon now, and who is it going to bless next? There are too many holes."

Thomas's father replied, "Calm down. It may be a story, but it does not mean it is any less true."

"Well, if that's the case, maybe I will be the next king of Tronsel, and I will use my riches to make the land better."

"Maybe you will, Thomas, but for now, off to bed with you. Tomorrow we must be up before dawn. It's harvest time, and we need the food, or I fear we will go hungry before winter arrives."

"Father, just one question before I go to bed."

"Yes, son, what is it?"

"Has anyone actually seen the golden dragon in real life?" Thomas asked.

"Some men have claimed to see a golden light fly through the night sky while others claim to see a beautiful woman with eyes like diamonds, there one second then gone the next."

"So that's a no, then?" Thomas asked.

His father replied, "Hard to say, but I know if you search hard enough, one day the golden dragon may find you. Now get some sleep, son, and dream of the golden dragon."

"Yes, sir. Good night, Father."

"Good night, my son."

The next morning came, bright rays of sunlight lighting up the log cabin, and a subtle warmth filled the one-room cabin that Thomas's father had built with his bare hands.

Melony, Thomas's mother, was a beautiful and radiant woman who was also kind and caring to others. Unfortunately, the past year was hard on the small family as Melony was gripped by a vicious fever that sadly took her life. Thomas did what he could to help his grieving father, but he knew no matter how many chores he did and no matter how good he was, he could not heal his father's ailing heart.

"Get up, Thomas. It's time to work," Thomas's father said.

"Yes, sir, I'm awake."

Thomas got out of bed, put on his white shirt his mother made him, and his worn brown pants with holes in the knees. He then slid on his leather shoes that were made by his father. They were strong but not very comfortable. Alas, Thomas's family was very poor, and all the money they made came from the crops they grew. The family did, however, own four large acres of land, which also included a nearby stream of clean, fresh, cold water at any time of the year. After a long, hard day in the fields, Thomas loved to swim, drink, and play in the river. It was also a wonderful source of fish, and due to the various crops they grew, game itself was plentiful.

"Father, after we work today, can we play in the river?" Thomas asked.

"Not today, son. I have business in town. I'm trusting you to watch the fields and home while I go into town and sell some meat and vegetables to get us some coin to buy better materials for clothes and other things we need."

"Yes, sir," Thomas replied.

Thomas was a good boy who listened to his father's every word. After his mother died, he felt he owed his father that. But on this day, fate would test his luck and his trust. In the afternoon, Thomas's father took off into town, and Thomas put his feet up and rested.

"A long day of hard work deserves a little rest," Thomas said as he listened to the soft, cool breeze. Exhaustion overtook Thomas, and he drifted off to sleep.

He dreamed of one day working in the field when a large dragon, ten times bigger than his home and covered in golden scales, descended into his garden, tearing it to pieces. He looked at the dragon, then Thomas yelled, "You destroyed my father's crops! How will you atone for this?"

The dragon said, "Young lord, I have come to free you and your father from poverty. This land, as well as all others, will be yours. Take one of my scales, and with it, the wealth of the world."

Thomas reached out to take the scale only to find it was blazing hot like fire, and it burned him. He quickly awakened to discover the oil lamp his father had lit before leaving had fallen, and the small log cabin was quickly catching fire.

"I don't know what to do!" Thomas thought quickly and ran to the river with a small bucket. He quickly filled the bucket and ran back to the house, spilling it as he ran. After attempting this three more times, his father returned home and was horrified at the thought that Thomas was inside. He ran in to save Thomas, not knowing Thomas was outside. He yelled, "Thomas, Thomas, where are you, son?" but his words were drowned in the flames.

As Thomas tried one more time for water, he slipped and fell, hitting his head on a rock that barely saw the light of day, and was unconscious.

Hours later, Thomas awoke, now dizzy from the fall. He remembered his father and yelled, "Father, Father!" Alas, no reply. He screamed, "Father, where are you?" Again, no reply. As he wandered through the wreckage of his home, he tripped over what appeared to be a fallen log. However, after Thomas looked closer, he was horrified to see the burnt remains of his father clutching on to his pillow as if it were him.

Out of fear, grief, and sadness, Thomas ran from the house, tears falling like the flow of the river. He ran into the nearby forest until he couldn't run anymore.

"Aaaaaaahhhhhhhhhh!" Thomas screamed in sadness and anger and proceeded to beat a nearby tree until both his hands bled, and his arms were bruised the color of black olives. With mucus and tears all over his face, he threw up and fell near the river.

The next morning, Thomas was awakened by the sun, and he went into the river to drink and to clean himself. He wandered back to his old home and ate the vegetables in the garden until he looked like a little ball, fuller than he had ever been. As he rested and mourned his father, he thought about the golden dragon and cursed the thought, yelling, "Stupid dragon, you don't even exist! If you did, my father and mother would still be alive."

All this did was make Thomas angrier, so he grabbed a nearby shovel that he had left on the ground the day prior, went down behind the home, and began to dig. With more tears, he dug his father a proper grave, and with the utmost care, he placed his father in the hole and buried him properly.

"I can't live like this forever," Thomas exclaimed. "I am only eight years old. I can't take care of myself, or can I?" Thomas then took what he could from the home and the knowledge his father had instilled in him and headed into the forest to forge his own path.

C H A P T E R

2

MANY YEARS HAD passed since that fateful night, and Thomas had grown into a fine and handsome young man. Now at the young age of nineteen, Thomas could rival any man in looks alone. From the meager eight-year-old boy grew a six-foot giant of a man with arms the size of keg barrels, a stomach as flat and smooth as stone, and a back strong enough to haul twice as much as any horse and three times as long. His legs were powerful enough to cut down trees with a single kick.

"Oh boy, what a long day," Thomas said as he drank and washed in the river. "I can't wait to get back home and eat." Thomas picked up a giant boar and proceeded to a log cabin nearby. This was the home he built for himself. With a roaring fire in front and openings to let the air in, Thomas's cabin could rival a king's in luxury. With a giant bed made from feathers of all kinds of fowl to the bearskin blankets he lay with and big sacks of straw for pillows, he slept very well in any time of the year.

Over the years, Thomas had built a name for himself in trade, offering rare goods for reasonable prices. His most precious possession was a sword he traded for the hide of a lion and the skull of a mountain ram. This sword had no jewels nor gold, but the blade was so sharp it could cut down a row of trees in one swoop. In Thomas's hands, it was used for cutting, skinning, and several other uses. Thomas, like his father, was also well off, though not rich, and to this day he still cursed the golden dragon for his misfortunes. He cursed any other beliefs of wealth and grandeur.

"Tonight, I will feast, and tomorrow I will sell the rest in town and buy new leather and materials to fix the damned leak in my

5

roof." As night approached, Thomas sat by the fire outside; no fire was ever allowed under any circumstance in his home. If it got too cold, he would hunt game, make thicker clothes, and sleep in them. As he slept, he dreamed again of the golden dragon. This had been the same dream since the incident when he was a boy.

However, this time it was different. This time, it was not a golden dragon that visited him but a young woman whose face was as flawless as the snow, and her eyes sparkled in the sunlight like pure diamonds. She was fair and had a figure that could make any man her slave, even a king. Thomas did not know this woman and asked, "Miss, are you lost? Do you need some help?"

The woman replied, "I am looking for you, sir. Thomas Melview, right?"

He said, "My lady, I am Thomas Melview, but do not confuse me with those armor-clad so-called knights. I am not now nor will ever be anything more than a farmer."

The woman replied, "I am Narvaria. I am what you know and that which you sought. I have not sought you, and why is your name that name?" At this moment, the beautiful woman opened her hands, and a bright light shone into Thomas's eyes, blinding him. As he awakened, he looked around and realized it was the morning of the next day.

"The clouds look dark today," said Thomas. "I hope it does not rain while I am at the market." Thomas grabbed his wares and began to walk into town. The town market was not far from Thomas's home, though no one would know that considering he stayed deep in the forest. As he walked, he pondered the woman in his dream. *Who are you, and why do I see you all the time? Not that I am complaining*, he thought to himself. As he walked for what seemed like an hour or so, he heard the loud sounds of people in the distance.

The market was finally close. He shouted and broke into a run to the busy streets of Mordan village. Mordan village was where his father would go to trade his goods, and that's where Thomas was now. As he approached the old shop, he thought of his father, and a small tear rolled down his cheek.

I'll make you proud, Father, he thought. As he put away the wares and opened the shop for business, a dagger suddenly went flying straight at his head. The sharp blade barely missed Thomas and made a loud smack sound against the wooden beam in front of him.

"Your aim is still off, I see," Thomas said as he took the dagger and threw it in the direction of the shop owner next to him. Gerum yelped and ducked for safety as the dagger clanged against some armor right by his head.

"Hahaha, my old friend, your aim is as sharp as my blades. As always, it is good to see you, brother," Gerum exclaimed.

Gerum was a drifter, so no one really knew where he came from or how long he had been in Mordan. But after the fire, Gerum was there to help Thomas get back on his feet. Gerum was a weapon and armor maker, and a fine one at that, for his wares were valued worldwide.

"How are you today, brother?" Gerum asked Thomas.

"I'm okay, brother, just haven't been sleeping well lately."

"Nightmares of the fire?" Gerum asked.

"Not so much. It's mainly of a woman," Thomas explained.

"Oh really?" Gerum gave Thomas a funny look. "A beautiful lady for my big strong brother, eh? Hahaha."

Gerum was not a big man. No one really knew how old he was, as he said he was older than time but looked like a young man. Gerum was short, only coming up to Thomas's chest in height, and frail almost to the bone. With pointy ears and a long spear-shaped nose, he joked it became flattened when it got wedged between two breastplates and stayed that way. His eyes were always red; he claimed it was from the soot and dust of the shop. He had a wheezy voice but overall had been Thomas's one true friend ever since the fire.

"What are you selling today, brother?" Thomas asked.

"Well, see for yourself, brother," Gerum said. "I've got new armor and a few new weapons for sale. But what about you? What did you bring from your forest abode? Hahaha."

"I've brought this," Thomas said, whipping out a pair of clothes made of lion's pelt and a very rare pair of boar's pelt shoes.

When it came to business, both Thomas and Gerum were the best of the best. Even though they could sell anywhere in the kingdom, they chose to stay close to home so people from the poor locals to rich noblemen of nearby kingdoms would flock to buy their wares. The two men were business rivals and business partners. While Gerum's weapons and armor were the best of the best, Thomas's pelts and clothes matched the quality point for point in every category.

The day started as usual for Thomas—busy, busy, busy.

"How much for the lamb shirt and deer pants?" one customer shouted.

"Three gold coins," Thomas shouted back.

"What about the bull-hide boots and cowhide pants?" another customer shouted.

"Five gold coins," Thomas shouted back.

The day was long, and the street was bustling with the roar of eager customers. Finally, after a whole day of dealing, haggling, and selling, the sun was starting to go down over the town. Thomas, after selling the very last of his wares, finally closed the shop around the same time as Gerum.

"How did you fare today, brother?" Thomas asked Gerum.

"Oh, my back! I swear, brother, if I had one more customer, I might have collapsed due to exhaustion."

"How did your fortune fare?" Gerum asked Thomas.

"Fifty thousand gold coins, enough to last throughout the winter and then some. And yourself?"

"I got forty-eight thousand. Not too bad, but as you said, enough and then some. It's been a great day for profit for both of us."

"I agree. Tell you what, let's go to Raven Tavern and drink our pain away—my treat," said Thomas.

"You read my mind, brother, and who knows? Maybe I'll find a lady as beautiful as the one you speak of all the time."

"Hahaha, I think you need to wash up before we go. Your greasy long jet-black hair is all gray from the ash. You look like an old troll. Hahaha."

"Oh, yeah? You think you're funny? Well, you smell like a dead animal and are covered in fur. You should sell yourself for a price. Hahaha."

The two laughed hysterically while picking on each other for about another hour as they rested from the day.

"You're right, though," Thomas said. "Come, let's wash by my river, and we will come back to drink."

"Sounds good to me, brother," and the two walked back to Thomas's river to wash up.

In the setting sun, the cool water of the river felt like a bath for kings.

"Ah, this is amazing," Gerum shouted. "Nothing is better than a cool bath after a long hot day, eh, brother?" Gerum said.

But Thomas did not respond.

"Thomas, Thomas, *Thomas*!" Gerum shouted.

"What?" replied Thomas.

"Are you feeling okay? It's like you're under a spell," Gerum asked.

"Oh, yeah, I'm fine. I just can't stop thinking about the woman," Thomas said.

"Well, if you love her so much, find her and marry her," Gerum explained.

"You don't understand," Thomas said. "I want to kill her."

"What! Kill her? Why?" Gerum asked.

"Because, Gerum, this woman is supposed to be the golden dragon my father praised so highly, and where was she when he was killed? Nowhere! I want to find her and kill her. I blame her for my father's death."

Anger swelled up in Thomas's heart so much so it was as if the water around him was starting to boil.

"Easy, brother, I was merely making a suggestion. There is no reason to get all angry at someone who does not exist."

"You're right, Gerum. I should not worry over a dream woman. Hahaha. I almost lost my head. Thank you, brother."

"Anytime," Gerum said. "Now let's get out of this water before we both fall asleep in it and freeze to death."

Thomas agreed, and they both went back to Thomas's home to change.

"Here, brother, I have something for you. You made me this sword a year ago, and now I have something for you. It's a full set."

Gerum was amazed, for Thomas had pulled out a shirt made of the finest silk, as if it were spun by the silkworms themselves. He also gifted two gauntlets made of horse hide and encrusted with jewels. The pants were lion's pelt, stylish, durable, and like wearing a cloud. Finally, there were boots made from a Tamarian bull, soft as fur but harder than metal.

Gerum paused at the sight of the clothes and began to cry, for no one had ever gifted him such magnificent clothes.

"Brother, I cannot take this. It is too much."

"Please, I insist," said Thomas.

"Okay, on one condition: you let me fashion your new armor. I promise it will be the finest in the whole kingdom."

Thomas agreed.

"Let's skip the tavern tonight and drink here," said Gerum.

"You know me, brother, I won't complain," and the two men drank all night.

The next day, it was dark and raining. The men awoke around noon with their heads pounding like war drums.

"Oh, my head," said Gerum.

"Mine as well," said Thomas.

Both men got up and noticed something different with Thomas's home.

"It's gone," said Thomas. "My home is gone!"

"Calm down, brother. We must have drunk too much and passed out. Let's find the road, and from there, we can get home."

"Okay, you're right."

As they began to move through the forest, Gerum shouted, "Hey, I have an idea—let's eat."

"Eat? But how? We have no weapons," Thomas explained with a puzzled look on his face.

"I have my dagger."

Gerum pulled out the dagger he threw at Thomas.

Thomas said, "Oh yeah, I forgot about that."

"Breakfast will be fast," Thomas exclaimed as the two men began to walk again.

Suddenly, in the clearing, a large deer was spotted by Gerum.

"Look, brother, over there," he whispered to Thomas, pointing to the deer in the clearing.

Thomas's eyes sharpened at the sight. His stomach ached, and he took the dagger and said, "Breakfast is served."

Thomas moved fast and quietly to the clearing, not arousing the deer. With a whoosh, he threw the dagger, piercing the heart of the deer faster than an arrow. The deer fell, and Thomas quickly finished the deer. Thomas's hunting prowess was on par with the king's royal knights, so by the time he returned with the deer in hand, Gerum already had a fire waiting.

Thomas cleaned the deer so precisely that blood almost never existed, it seemed. Gerum cooked the deer like a master chef, and they both ate in silence. After their bellies were full, their wits also returned, and Thomas knew exactly where they were.

"Why, brother," he said to Gerum, "we're only a mile or so south of my home we can be there by the time the sun is above us."

"Sounds good to me!" Gerum shouted in excitement.

They quickly made for a sprint, Gerum following Thomas. As they ran, it looked like two shadows flying in the woods. Thomas got his speed from chasing down animals while Gerum got his speed from moving red-hot metal. They both moved like pure lightning. After what seemed like mere seconds, the two arrived at Thomas's home and took a good rest.

Thomas made some boar stew and vegetables as Gerum laid out the plans for Thomas's armor.

"This will take a year," Gerum explained.

"Brother, again, it's not necessary," Thomas tried to say, but Gerum laughed.

"Okay, fine, you win," Thomas said.

After a while, the stew was ready. They both ate, laughed, and expressed merriment for what seemed like hours. By this time, the sun had set, and Gerum said, "Brother, I must be getting home. As much as staying here is always a pleasure, I must get back to work, as should you."

Thomas agreed and hugged his brother.

"Be careful going home, and I will see you next year at the market."

"You do the same, and I will have your armor by the next market."

They hugged again as Gerum walked off. After Gerum was out of sight, Thomas went to bed and hoped he did not dream of the now-evil witch known as Narvaria.

C H A P T E R

3

IT HAD BEEN one year since the last market, and Thomas grew more handsome by the day, now sporting a fashionable majestic beard and mustache. He set out for the famous town market.

I hope I can sell some of the furs I have this year. I don't need twelve deer pelts and fifteen elk pelts. I traveled far in search of exotic animals, and boy, was I rewarded. It has been a good year. Thomas surprisingly did not have any dreams of Narvaria and had almost forgotten about her, but the night of his father's demise and the story he told about her remained.

"Good morning, my old friend," Thomas roared to Gerum.

"Good morning, brother. It's good to see you!" Gerum shouted. Gerum looked different now, sporting muscle and looking full of life.

"You look good, my friend," Thomas said.

"Well, it has been a busy and good year. Come, I have a surprise for you."

"Of course, but first, allow me time to set up my shop. I will be over in a few minutes."

"Not a problem. Why don't I help you to make it easier and faster?" Gerum asked.

"I would like that, thank you. By the way, I have something for you. It is clothes made from dragon skin. I found a baby dragon, and with this, it should not be so hot next to the fire as the clothes repel it."

"No." Gerum winced, almost in anger. "I cannot take this. It's too rare," he said, and his eyes began to turn dark. "Never mind, brother. I just don't think I'm worthy of it, that's all. Thank you for the gift. I will wear it every time I work."

"My friend, you are far more worthy of it than me, but enough talk. Let's work, what do you say?" Thomas asked.

"Yes, let's set you up and then you can see my gift. I told you it would take a year, and I finished it last night. I'm sure you will be pleased."

"I always am, brother." Gerum and Thomas worked quickly and diligently, and before long, Thomas's shop was open for business.

There were people lined up to enter both shops, and the crowd bustled as the two merchants made fast trades and fast deals. By nightfall, the two were exhausted; their shops looked like they almost had nothing to offer anyone, but their coin purses were, as always, about to burst at the seams with coins. In fact, that is exactly what Thomas's did.

Rrrriiippp! The coin purse Thomas had on his side ripped open with a ferocious noise.

"Oh no!" Thomas yelled as his coins fell to the floor and rolled all over his shop in an attempt to escape Thomas. "My coins! I can't carry all of this. What am I going to do?"

"Brother, what happened?" Gerum asked.

"My coin purse busted," said Thomas.

"Don't worry, brother, I have a solution to this. Do you still have the dragon skin shirt?"

"Yes, but that is yours. I made it for you," Thomas answered.

"True, but consider this a gift from me. I will keep the pants, and you make the shirt into a new coin purse. Dragons have been known to hoard treasure, right? So don't you think it is fitting that a dragon hoards your treasure? Hahahaha!"

Thomas also laughed in a hysterical manner. "You're right, Gerum. I will get on it right away. It should not take more than an hour to complete."

"Great, I will gather the coins for you, and after we're done, you can treat me to a round or ten at the tavern. Sound good?" Gerum said, laughing.

"Of course," Thomas answered, also laughing. "All rounds are on me tonight."

"Hmm." In a tired tone, Thomas finally spoke, "It's done." That dragon skin shirt had been conformed to a large sack that was double-stitched to support more coins than before.

"Great!" Gerum shouted. "All this running around has made me thirsty!" Gerum shouted as he collected the last two coins.

The very last coin Gerum touched turned a dark purple color, then back to its original. Gerum smiled sinisterly at this revelation. "I have them, brother," he said as he brought the last two coins to Thomas, who eagerly put them in his new dragon skin purse. The new purse could hold all the coins from the day and double that with ease. Thomas was very pleased with his work.

"Let's go Gerum drinks are on me as promised."

"After you, my lord, hahaha," Gerum said, opening the door sarcastically and bowing as if to refer to Thomas as a great king.

Thomas laughed and replied, "Thank you, squire. You're most kind."

Gerum laughed as they both left the shop together and headed for the mead tavern in the center of town.

As soon as the two approached the door and entered, the owner shouted, "Look, everyone, it's Thomas and Gerum!"

A deafening "huzzah!" bellowed from every individual in reverence for the two craftsmen.

"Mr. Bostic, how goes thee?" Thomas asked.

Mr. Bostic, the tavern owner, was a man in his seventies and built like a small barkeep. He was soft but stern with his words.

"You boys have really helped this town ever since you two came to sell your fine wares during the market. Our town has had many new customers from all over, and revenue has been the highest in years! We all owe you boys a great deal, so tonight drinks are on us. As many as you like. What do you all say?" Mr. Bostic yelled at the crowd.

"Huzzah!" shouted the crowd.

"Then it's settled. You two drink for free."

"Thank you, Mr. Bostic and everyone here!" Gerum shouted. "A mug of ale for Thomas and me."

"Coming right up!" Mr. Bostic yelled and went to make the drinks.

Seconds later, he returned with two giant mugs that a normal man would need two hands to hold, full of foamy ale. Gerum looked concerned but tipped it back nonetheless. Thomas did the same and took a huge gulp of ale.

"This is fantastic," Thomas shouted. "Please, Mr. Bostic, let me pay you, sir."

"I said no, boy," Mr. Bostic yelled at Thomas with a mean look. "You boys are heroes, and I will not take any payment from you, and that is that."

"Yes, sir," Thomas answered. "But at least let me give you this." Thomas opened out three gold coins from his purse.

"I will accept these only so that you don't talk about payment the whole night. Deal?"

"Deal," Thomas answered.

That night, Thomas and Gerum drank and were merry with the whole town. By morning, they were so hungover that the only thought on their minds was food.

"Thomas, are you awake?" Gerum asked.

"Yes, brother, I'm up. My head is spinning," Thomas replied.

"As is mine. Let's get some food at Madam Dobreigh's bakery."

"Fresh baked rolls do sound good. Let's go."

As they left the store, Thomas noticed the town was destroyed.

"I wonder what happened," said Thomas.

"I don't know. Let's get over to Madam Dobreigh's bakery quick."

Upon arriving at the bakery, the two noticed it was in shambles and Madam Dobreigh was nowhere to be found.

"Thomas, quick, we must find someone and ask what has happened!" Gerum yelled.

"I agree, but where are we going to look? The town is deserted," Thomas said.

"What about old man Dockens, who lives on the outskirts of town? He never leaves his home," Gerum said.

"You're right. Let's go," Thomas shouted.

Upon arriving at Dockens' home, they found the old man holding tight to a pitchfork and shaking wildly.

"Mr. Dockens," Thomas said, "sir, are you all right?"

"The beast…the beast destroyed the town and took Madam Dobreigh!"

"The beast? What beast?" Gerum said. "Tell us, sir, what beast?"

"It was giant. It had two heads. One was that of a wild dog with a boar's snout and huge tusks, with dog ears and thick black fur. The other smaller head looked like Mr. Bostic, with missing teeth and a bloodcurdling tongue falling from his mouth. It walked on four legs and was eight feet tall! Its arms were all of different animals: one human, another a spider's leg, another a scorpion's claw, and its last was a writhing bloody tentacle. All the limbs, including a tail, had bone spikes jutting from everywhere. It almost made me vomit!" Mr. Dockens said.

"But that was not the worst part, boys. It had wings like a dragon, and in the canine mouth was Ms. Dobreigh's mangled body. As it left the town, I came out to see the destruction it had caused. As I looked at it, the head that looked like Mr. Bostic said my name in a rusty, gurgling noise as it flew off to who knows where. I have been on guard ever since, waiting for it to come back for me!" Mr. Dockens said.

As he spoke, the two just stared at him in shock about this story he was telling them.

"Don't worry. We are here now," Thomas said to Mr. Dockens.

"Yes, we will find and kill this monster, Mr. Dockens," Gerum said.

"You boys, the town owes you a great deal of thanks."

"Let's go, Gerum," Thomas said.

"Wait, brother. We need to go back to my shop."

"What for?" Thomas asked.

"Remember, I promised you a suit of armor, and I have delivered. So what better time to use it?" Gerum explained.

"Oh yeah, I forgot. Let's go see," and they took off for Gerum's shop.

Upon arriving, Gerum said, "Wait here, as it will be a little overwhelming. This is my finest work yet."

"Okay, I'll wait at the door," Thomas answered. Soon Gerum pulled out a chest big enough to house a king's royal jewels and opened the chest to reveal a blinding golden light. After the sunlight was redirected from the armor, Thomas could see its true beauty.

The helmet was gold, with two majestic horns on the sides and a royal dragon symbol in the center. The breastplate had beautiful stones of diamonds, rubies, and sapphires on the arms, edges, and torso with another dragon in the front. The gauntlets supported stones on the wrist and elbow edges of jade. And finally, the golden leggings, which at the ankle, knees, and thigh edges supported onyx stones. It was truly a golden armor set fit for a god.

"Unbelievable, brother! This is truly your finest work yet. I am speechless."

"Well, I do try for my family after all. Now try it on quickly. We're running out of time, and we still need to get to both your home and mine."

"Agreed," Thomas said, and he donned the armor.

First, the leggings fit better than his own clothes, and he felt as if he could outrun the fastest animal in the world. Next were the gauntlets, which made his muscles feel like they were going to burst with power and that he could lift a mountain. The breastplate made him feel invincible, as if nothing and no one could do him harm. And finally, the helmet fit perfectly, and through it, he could see clearer than before, almost as if with the helmet he could see great distances in perfect clarity, and his mind felt open to the universe itself.

"This armor is amazing, Gerum. Are you sure I can really have this?" Thomas asked.

"Of course. I told you it's yours, but there's no time for admiration now. As we speak, that monster is getting further away from us."

"You're right. Let's go to your place so you can get ready."

"Agreed," Gerum replied, and they headed for Gerum's home.

Gerum's home was not far, as he lived in town, hence why he always beat Thomas to market every year.

"We're here!" Gerum shouted and ran into his home while Thomas waited outside.

Within minutes, Gerum came out and looked as if he was a blacksmith clown. His head sported a leather cap with big magnifying glass lenses and a feather. His arms had no armor, but big, thick soot-covered gloves, and his pants were the dragon skin pants Thomas made, followed by a pair of big iron boots. Upon Gerum's back was a big sack full of blacksmithing tools and ores. His weapon was a simple single-shot crossbow and a small dagger on his side.

Thomas laughed. "Are you sure you want to go on a hunt like this Gerum? You could be killed" Thomas asked.

"Oh no, dear brother. I'm not going into battle—you are. I'm coming as your blacksmith. I can make and repair your equipment for you and keep it in tip-top shape."

Gerum replied, "You're right. You will actually be better than having another warrior by my side. If you're truly ready, brother, then we can make it to my house by nightfall."

"I am, brother," Gerum promised, and they left for Thomas's home in the woods on the outside of town.

Upon arriving, Thomas noticed the smoke from his home was much thicker than usual. "Oh no!" he shouted as he took off like a bolt of lightning. He arrived at his home too late, however, and all he found was rubble. He clenched his fists so tight they began to bleed as he heard the words, "Thomas, my boy," from what sounded like a dying animal. He paused, listening for the sound, and soon discovered the remains of Madam Dobreigh barely clinging to life.

"Ms. Dobreigh, thank God you're alive. What happened?"

By this time, Gerum had arrived at the house as well and started looking through the rubbish in shock at what had happened. He walked aimlessly until he found a shining golden sword lying in the wreckage.

Before he could pick it up, he heard Thomas shout, "Gerum, Ms. Dobreigh is here!" Gerum quickly stopped what he was doing and ran toward Thomas and Ms. Dobreigh. To the boys' horror, Ms. Dobreigh had been ripped to pieces, with chunks of bone, blood, and organs scattered as if she was a dog's chew toy.

"Boys, listen," Ms. Dobreigh said as the boys remained silent. "Mr. Bostic somehow turned into this thing last night. I believe it was dark magic, the darkest, most evil kind. I tried to talk to him, but he only cried, and the monster took me in its jaws and ran away with me. You must be careful, Thomas. I feel dark venom from the monster's horrid mouth in my body, and I am going to die here. Please save Mr. Bostic for me and free his soul. I die having no regrets."

She spoke her final words. Both Thomas and Gerum had looked at Ms. Dobreigh as a mother figure, so they both were overcome with grief, crying for a long time. After giving her a burial fit for a queen, Thomas said, "We need to find this monster and free Mr. Bostic if there is a way to free him.

Gerum said, "Yes, but how? We don't know where the beast has gone."

"Well, judging from these tracks in my home and the blood trail leaving the home, I would say it headed west to the Cogham Mountains."

"Those mountains are dangerous, Thomas. No man goes up there because of the stories."

"What stories?" Thomas asked.

"You know, the stories of the three troll brothers that control the road to the peak of the mountains."

"Oh, yeah, I have heard of them—Tremous, Doscare, and Brutilis, right?" Thomas asked.

"Yes, no man has ever bested them. Besides, they say a river goddess and an old monk live on the mountain. Supposedly, it's home to you-know-who," Gerum stated.

"No, I don't, Gerum. Who lives there and is so profound to be protected?" Thomas asked.

"Well, you know…Narvaria."

"What the fuck did you say?" Thomas shouted in anger. "That witch of a dragon supposedly lives there, and I am finding this out now? Why did you not tell me sooner?" Thomas shouted.

Gerum replied, "I did not tell you for these reasons. One, it's only a myth. Two, you are irritable and hot-tempered. And three, you would die before you even got to the foot of the mountain, let alone the peak.

"Look, Thomas, along the path following the blood trail leads to Raddigon Forest. In the forest lies Brutilis, the craftiest of the troll brothers. They say no man has resisted his mind manipulation."

"Well then, let's set off," Thomas said as he grabbed the golden hilt of his sword, sheathed it, and said, "and put these myths to the ultimate test."

4

"WE'VE BEEN WALKING for hours, Gerum, and it seems like we're going in circles," Thomas commented.

"Well, we don't have a map, Thomas, and it's not like I can make a map of the area magically appear," Gerum retorted.

Thomas and Gerum had been walking through the forest and were indeed lost. Little did they know, they were on the right track and already caught by Brutilis's mind control.

You fools, another helpless duo caught by my mind labyrinth trap. They will walk in circles until they die of exhaustion, then I will devour them and steal all they are holding. Hahahahaha, what a perfect plan, Brutilis gloated.

Brutilis watched for hours, seeing the pair walk in a circle aimlessly until he started to feel tired.

Yyyyaaawwwwnnnn. "I'm getting sleepy watching them. It's been hours, and they haven't rested yet. I'm going to take a quick nap. Who knows, maybe when I wake up, they will be dead," Brutilis said to himself.

As Brutilis slept, Thomas and Gerum were getting tired and frustrated with each other.

"You have no idea where we're going, do you?" Gerum shouted at Thomas.

"Well, I would if you weren't nagging me every five seconds!" Thomas shouted back.

The two argued for what seemed like hours until Thomas stood up from a sitting position with a loud, "That's it, Gerum."

Thomas picked up a large stick and threw it at Gerum's head. Gerum ducked with insane speed.

"Are you crazy, Thomas? The exhaustion has your wits, brother. Take this." Gerum grabbed a rock and threw it at Thomas's head. Thomas ducked just in time.

"Why, you—that's enough, brother!" Thomas shouted as he prepared to fight Gerum.

"Wait, brother!" Gerum yelled, and Thomas stopped to listen.

"Brother, do you hear that?" Gerum said.

"Hear what?" Thomas asked.

"Exactly," Gerum said. "You tossed that log with extensive force, yet it did not make a sound, and I threw that rock with all my strength, yet it still has not made a sound. Why do you think that is?"

"I don't know," Thomas replied.

"Don't you get it, brother? We are on the right track. We've been on the right track this whole time. We're caught in a spell."

"A spell?" Thomas looked around in surprise. "You're right. Everything is quiet—no trees, no wind, no birds even—and we have been walking around for hours. Gerum, you're a genius, brother. I'm sorry for my actions. Can you forgive me?"

"Already forgiven, brother. Now we have to figure out how to get out of here," Gerum explained.

"I have an idea," Thomas said. "If this is a mind spell, that means Brutilis is near. If we can shake him up somehow from in here, maybe he will lose his focus and we will be free."

"That is a great idea, brother, but how?" Gerum asked.

"I have an idea. The rock and the log had to go somewhere, right? What if we started throwing objects outside of the barrier and see what happens?" Thomas explained.

"Worth a shot," Gerum retorted. "After all, it's better than doing nothing. We will die in here if we do not do something."

Thomas and Gerum began to throw stones and logs in every direction.

After a few throws, Brutilis was woken up by a large log hitting his head.

"Eh, ah, what the hell?" As his blurry eyes tried to focus, he screamed, "Ooowww! My head! What hit me?"

Finally, his eyes came into focus to reveal a sword at his neck and a crossbow at his head.

"Get up, Brutilis the troll," Thomas yelled. "Your head will be mine after what you did. You deserve to die."

"Waaaaiiiitttt! Wait, Sir Thomas, you don't understand."

"I am not a knight. Do not call me sir, troll."

"Of course, Master Thomas," Brutilis answered. "You don't understand. I am here as a guard to test you on your journey from the great black dragon."

"Black dragon? What black dragon, Brutilis?" Thomas asked.

"His name is Zerok. I do not know his true face, but I serve him. He knows of your travels and is out to stop you," Brutilis explained. "That's all I know, Master Thomas. Honest, no, please let me live, master."

"Well, have I passed your test, Brutilis?"

"Yes, master, but there is one more thing. Take *this*."

As Brutilis shouted, he threw a bottle on the ground and disappeared. The clouds became dark, and out of nowhere, a ten-foot monster was born.

"Behold my true form!" Brutilis shouted as he sat on two demonic legs with spikes protruding from the knees. His torso was tight and muscular as steel, and his arms that were meek and frail before now sported massive claws for fingers, spikes protruding from the elbows. His head, which had previously been an average warty cranium, was now a massive brain pulsating almost out of his skull. His pointy ears had become batwing-like and fused to his head, and his eyes and teeth were both bloodred and huge.

"Now you die, human!" Brutilis lunged forward and slashed at Gerum with his mighty claws. Gerum quickly dodged and shot an arrow that bounced off Brutilis's massive pulsating brain.

"That is not good enough, human!" Brutilis shouted.

Thomas quickly cut off Brutilis's left arm with a loud whoosh.

"Aaaaahhh!" Brutilis shouted in pain as purple blood came pouring out.

"Give up, Brutilis. You can't beat the both of us."

"Oh, really, fool? I have already won."

Thomas looked in horror as Brutilis's arm grew back while the other arm grew a new body.

"Cut all you want, fools. I'll keep coming back!"

"This won't work," Gerum said to Thomas.

"I know, but what other choice do we have?"

"Let's try stabbing and shooting for his heart," Gerum explained.

"I'll try anything at this point," Thomas said.

"Quit your whining and give up!" Brutilis used his telekinetic power to pick up logs and stones and began to throw them at the duo. "You can't win."

Brutilis charged like a wild beast.

"Thomas, now!" Gerum shouted. Thomas quickly lunged at Brutilis, and his sword pierced his heart. Brutilis screamed as blood poured from his mouth.

"It's over, Brutilis." Thomas turned the sword to end the beast quickly, only to discover the other two monsters vanished into thin air, and all that remained was the frail first form of Brutilis with a blade in his head.

Thomas quickly pulled his sword as the illusion faded. "Damn, I now have more questions. Who is this Zerok, and why does he want me stopped? Gerum, are you alive back there?" he asked.

"Yes, one moment, Thomas, then we can get going." Gerum bent down to the corpse of Brutilis and mumbled a spell. Suddenly, the corpse exploded in powerful light, and a ghostlike figure appeared from the body. Gerum then pointed to Thomas and shouted, "Rekombeknox," and the soul flew into the armor.

Thomas' mind was instantly invigorated by the soul. "You know magic, Gerum?" Thomas asked in shock.

"Only that one spell I learned many years ago. It transfers the souls of the dead into armor and weapons to invigorate the user with a special skill."

"Who taught you this spell?" Thomas asked.

"My old master," Gerum replied.

In confusion, Thomas's head began to pound. "My head feels like it's burning, Gerum," Thomas said as he rolled on the ground in pain.

"That's just your mind adapting to it. Don't fight it, brother. Let it wash over you and engulf you in its power."

Thomas relaxed and felt power flow through his mind to the rest of his body.

When he opened his eyes again, it seemed nothing had changed. However, when he sat up, he noticed stones and twigs of trees were floating in midair.

"Hahahahaha, that's it, brother! You have gained Brutilis's power of telekinesis. Go on, try it out," Gerum yelled excitedly.

Telekinesis, Thomas thought as he looked at his hand and then at a nearby tree. While pointing his hand, he shouted, "Up, tree!" The massive tree began to shake. Concentrating harder, he said, "Up, tree!" His head began to hurt, but the tree broke free from its roots in a massive burst of power. Thomas sent the giant tree flying and blacked out immediately after.

When Thomas woke back up, night had arrived. Gerum had made a fire and was roasting some very succulent meat and savory vegetable soup he had made.

"You overdid it. New powers are great, but they take a toll on the user. Come, brother, eat."

Thomas, without saying a word, came to the fire and made himself a hearty bowl. The aroma was mouthwatering, and the taste was divine.

"How did you learn to cook so well, brother?"

"I taught myself when I was a boy, just like you. Now let's eat and rest so we can get back to the journey tomorrow."

"I agree," Thomas answered with a mouth full of food. "Just one more thing, Gerum." The tension became stiff between the two. "What do you know about this great black dragon Brutilis spoke of?"

"I don't know. Maybe an excuse from a man about to die," Gerum explained. "I've never heard of a black dragon of any kind, but hey, if one does exist, we will kill it too, eh?"

"You're right," Thomas laughed, and they ate happily. Finally, with full bellies, they lay by the fire and fell fast asleep.

The next morning, the duo was awakened by rainfall and a loud yell.

5

Rrrrrrrooooooaaaaarrrrr!

"What on earth was that?" Gerum shouted as they scrambled to get out of the rain.

"I don't know," Thomas responded. "Sounded like it came from the foot of the mountain."

Suddenly, a huge boulder was flying at sonic speed toward Gerum.

"Move!" shouted Thomas as Gerum turned to face the boulder. The boulder hit the ground with a sickening smash, and Thomas looked on in horror as it seemed like Gerum was crushed.

"*Gerum!*"

"I'm okay, brother. It barely missed me—Watch out!" Gerum shouted as another boulder smashed into a nearby tree, barely missing Thomas.

"We have to get out of here!" shouted Thomas.

"I agree!" Gerum shouted back.

"We can run to that clearing beside us," Thomas said, and they ran as fast as they could. They discovered a clearing of trees and were safe from the boulders for now.

"What in the kingdom was that?" Thomas asked.

"I don't know, but it did not like us," Gerum stated. "Well, we are safe here for now," Gerum said grimly.

"Why so glum, brother? We're here, we're both safe, and we're both alive. There's no need to be glum."

"I'm afraid so, brother. If I'm right, that roar and those boulders were connected," Gerum replied.

"You mean there is a monster strong enough to lift a mountain-sized boulder and throw it at us?"

"Yes, I believe it is Tremous, the second, brother, and physically the strongest of the three," Gerum replied.

"Okay, can you tell me more about the trolls?" Thomas asked incredulously.

"Yes, and each one is deadlier than the last. You see, Brutilis was the strongest mind of the three. Tremous can move mountains and is a mindless brute. He only cares about strength and combat. And then there is Doscare, the oldest troll. He is the most powerful magic user in the kingdom. No one is his equal in magic as a whole."

Great, Thomas thought, *More problems and we've only begun this journey.*

"Okay, so where would Tremous be hiding then Gerum?"

"Don't worry, he is not hiding. He lives at the foot of the mountain path. He hides for no one."

"Then we should be off, brother, before he finds us and decides to crush us again," Thomas suggested.

"There is no need, brother. Tremous is simple, and with the rain, it could be hours before he finds us again. Especially if the rain holds, he won't be able to match our sound with the rain blocking it out."

"Good. I will use this time to practice my new telekinesis gift. What are you going to do, Gerum?"

"Finish my sleep, Thomas. After all, I know I'm going to be very busy if we face Tremous."

"I hope not. I'm beginning to like this armor." Thomas laughed.

"Hey, I can always take it back," Gerum said, sporting a smile.

"No thanks, brother. A gift like this I will wear all my life," Thomas retorted with a smile.

"Please don't," Gerum said, laughing. "I don't need you stinking it up. If you die, I won't be able to sell it if it smells like burnt arse."

They both laughed as Thomas turned around and Gerum lay down and drifted back to sleep under the trees while it continued to rain.

After a while, Thomas still did not feel tired, so he thought of an idea. He began training his new mental power by starting with small stones and twigs. After four hours, he was almost a master of the art. He could make stones and small boulders float around with little to no effort and move trees and boulders the size of a wagon with more concentration and effort, without fainting from exhaustion.

As Gerum awoke, the rain had stopped, and the sun was beginning to peak from the clouds. Thomas killed a deer using his telekinesis by throwing a large stone at its head. He then made a fire and cooked the meat with some roots and herbs he had found while training.

"That smells amazing," Gerum said as he woke up and moved to the fire to dry from the rain.

"Ah, you're awake. About time, brother," Thomas exclaimed.

"Yes, well, unlike you, I can't sleep through the world ending," Gerum retorted while grabbing a bowl from his bag.

Thomas and Gerum ate and drank water from their water jugs. As darkness began to fall, Gerum said, "When nightfall approaches, we can get moving. Tremous sleeps at night, so if we sleep during the day and move at night, we can reach the foot of the mountain undetected. But be warned, Tremous is a giant of a troll. He towers as high as a large castle and has muscles all over his body as smooth as stone and as hard as pure iron. If we can get by him, we should be able to avoid conflict."

Thomas, looking deep in thought, said, "I agree. If we are to survive the journey, let's get moving. When we get to the foot of the mountain, we will make a better decision on what to do."

As the two began to move, they ran quickly, taking small breaks along the path to rest. They arrived halfway to the foot of the mountain by the time the sun appeared over the horizon.

"Let's stop here, Thomas," Gerum said with a tired voice.

"Yes, this is a good place to rest. We also need to recover our food and water. Let's go off the path and set up camp."

They had traveled off the path for about a mile when they came to a beautiful field of flowers.

"This area will be good to mask our scents. As we are so close to the foot, Tremous will surely smell us from here, so these flowers will help hide our scent," Gerum explained while they laid down their gear and divided the workload.

"I will go hunting," Thomas exclaimed.

"Okay, I will get water, and we both shall get herbs that we find along the way," Gerum said in a tired voice.

They both set out, and after an hour's time, they returned. Thomas had caught a wild boar and gathered many plants and roots to eat. Gerum had found a clean river and restocked their water supply with fresh water. He also found herbs to aid with sleep and recovery from injuries.

"Let's cook and eat, brother," said Thomas as he cut the meat. It was midday when they ate their fill and lay down to sleep in the shade of the flowers and trees.

By nightfall, both awoke refreshed and smelled like the flowers they had laid in.

"Ready, Thomas?" Gerum asked as he picked up the heavy load and put it on his back.

"I'm ready," Thomas exclaimed as he did the same. "If we keep moving at the pace we are, we will arrive at the foot of the mountain by daybreak, and from there, we might be able to slip past Tremous and make our way up the mountain to the peak."

"Sounds good to me," Thomas said. "I will race you!" And like a bolt of lightning, Thomas ran back on the path, leaving Gerum in a trail of dust.

"I don't think so, brother!" Gerum took off, matching Thomas in speed.

They quickly arrived at the foot of the mountain just before daybreak.

"What is that horrible stench?" Thomas yelled as he clutched his nose.

"That, my friend, is Tremous." Just as Gerum pointed to a giant boulder, it suddenly moved, revealing a warty arm and what looked like hairy trees. The stench was overwhelming, and both of them backed away quickly.

"Oh my god, Thomas! He smells horrible. How are we going to get past that without dying from the smell alone?" Gerum asked.

"I don't know, but look, he's waking up," Thomas exclaimed.

A loud booming yawn came from the beast as Tremous rolled over and opened his eyes.

"Quick, hide, Thomas," Gerum said, and the two quickly ducked behind a boulder. They both tried to steal quick glances at the troll while holding in their gags.

Tremous was, as stated by Gerum, huge, with skin like onyx stone and as green as a swamp. His face was covered in warts, and he had a nose as big as a house and teeth that could crush stone. His fangs were cracked and chipped, and his ears were tiny, almost like a walnut on a tree. As he woke, he opened his mouth to reveal corpses stuck in his teeth that made his breath worse than death itself. His armpits looked like a dark abyss because of the hair and smelled as if one thousand pigs had died all at once and were rotting for weeks.

As Tremous looked around, he caught a whiff of something disgusting, "What is that?" he shouted. "Flowers! I hate flowers!" As he looked around, he began to smash everything in search of the horrid smell of flowers. "Where are those disgusting flowers?" Just then, an arrow went flying and poked his arm. It smashed into pieces against his hide. "I found you!" he shouted as he moved a huge boulder and discovered Thomas and Gerum hiding.

6

"Quick, run!" Thomas yelled as they scrambled to run away from the boulder Tremous slammed down to crush them.

"You can't hide from me!" Tremous yelled as he began to chase the duo.

"Maybe if we split up, it will confuse him!" Gerum yelled.

"That sounds like a great idea!" Thomas yelled back. "Aaaannnnddddd go split up!"

Gerum went left into the woods while Thomas stayed on the path.

"You can't hide from me!" Tremous screamed as he threw a huge stone at Thomas.

"Oh no!" yelled Thomas as he came to a quick stop. The stone slammed into the path right where he would have been standing if he had not stopped.

"I got you," Tremous shouted as he grabbed ahold of Thomas and began to squeeze the life from him like a snake squeezing the life from its prey.

Thomas, in agony, screamed, "Why do you hate us, great Tremous? We were only passing through!"

"Liar!" Tremous responded. "I smell dark magic on you, and my brother Brutilis's smell is on your armor. You killed him. I can feel it."

"He started it, and I am no dark magician, but I do have this." Just then, Thomas managed to free an arm and grab his sword. With a whoosh, Thomas cut Tremous's fingers clean off.

Tremous screamed in pain. "Why, you little worm! I'll kill you!"

Just then, an arrow flew into Tremous's eye, and he fell over in pain.

"Gerum!" Thomas shouted. "It'll work for a little while. Nice shot," Thomas praised.

"Eh, it was nothing, but a small wound like that won't keep him down for long. What are we going to do?" Gerum asked.

"I have an idea. Can you keep him occupied for a minute while I try something?"

"I'll do what I can, Thomas, but don't take long. Tremous's weak spot is his eyes. Your sword got lucky."

Just then, Tremous got up and locked eyes with Gerum. "You little runt, die." He grabbed Gerum and threw him the length of a large town. Gerum screamed the entire time and hit the ground hard. Rolling around, he was stopped dead by a tree and lost consciousness.

With only one eye, Tremous began to smell the air. "Where are you, swordsman?"

Suddenly, a small rock hit Tremous in the head with a thud. "What the hell was that?" As Tremous looked up, he noticed something blocking the sun but could not see what exactly because he only had one eye. It was hard to make out the object. "Wait, I smell blood and my brother." Tremous, bleeding from his nose and eyes, turned quickly and saw Thomas. "This is for you, Tremous. Die like your brother!"

Suddenly, the shadow of the object became fast and clear. Thomas had used his telekinesis to pick up a boulder the size of a mountain and place it high enough above Tremous to crush him entirely.

"Oh no!" Tremous screamed as he put both of his huge arms in the air to stop the boulder, but he forgot to regenerate the fingers on his left hand, the ones Thomas cut off.

Just then, the boulder slipped and slammed Tremous to the ground, crushing him with unbelievable force. Thomas blacked out and collapsed where he stood. The woods then became silent for what seemed like days.

As Thomas awoke, he saw Gerum standing over him.

"You okay, Thomas?" Gerum asked as a green light washed over Thomas.

"I'm okay, Gerum. What about you?"

"I'm okay after I got a lesson in flying, hitting a tree, and becoming, how do you say, intimate. Next thing I know, Tremous is dead, and so were you—or at least you looked dead," Gerum explained. "So I found a green potion in your bag and poured it down your throat. I hope that was okay," Gerum said in a worried voice.

Thomas sat up and said, "Yes, that was a healing potion my father taught me. It heals my wounds almost instantly. How long have I been asleep?"

"Two days," replied Gerum.

"That explains why Tremous smells worse now than before." Thomas laughed.

"Oh, yeah, that reminds me. Are you ready to eat? I have made food. I stayed by your side and made camp here while you were asleep."

"Yes, that sounds good," Thomas answered with a groan. "I feel so weak."

"Here, eat this," Gerum responded while handing Thomas a bowl of hot and steaming fresh soup. They ate and drank until they both were completely recovered.

"Aaaahhhhhh, that really hit the spot. Thank you, brother," Thomas said to Gerum.

"Don't mention it. By the way, are you ready for the soul power of Tremous?" Gerum asked.

"Yes, let's do this," said Thomas.

"Okay, here we go." Gerum began to chant and pointed at the armor. Suddenly, as before, a white light flew from Tremous and slammed into Thomas's armor.

Thomas was overwhelmed and moved back six steps before feeling the familiar wash of power come over him. "This is incredible," Thomas smiled and shouted. "I feel invincible. Oh my, what power!"

After the transfer was complete, Thomas felt fully energized and had to release it somehow. "I feel so powerful but have no idea what I received," said Thomas.

"Why don't you try picking something up, and we will see what happens," Gerum suggested.

"Okay," Thomas answered and walked over to the stone that crushed Tremous. With no effort, he picked up the massive boulder one-handed. "Wow, this feels like a twig in my hand. I feel as though I can crush it as easily as a weak old branch. This is truly an amazing power."

Gerum said, "Huzzah, that is wonderful because we will need all our strength for the final troll brother, Doscare."

"And where does he reside?"

"In a cave at the base, only one hundred meters above Tremous. You could say Tremous was his bodyguard," explained Gerum.

"If that's the case, then this will be easy," said Thomas.

"Don't get cocky, Thomas. Doscare has never been beaten in battle and has no equal in terms of magic. He will be incredibly difficult to defeat."

Thomas, confused, asked, "Is there any point on the way up to Narvaria's keep that does not have powerful enemies in our path?"

"Unfortunately not, I'm afraid," Gerum answered in a dreary tone.

"Okay, then let's go," said Thomas as he got up and prepared to move.

Suddenly, Thomas stopped moving and speaking and fell back to the ground with a loud thud. "Thomas, are you all right?"

"I don't know. I felt fine, then all of a sudden, I felt dizzy and confused. Next thing I know, I'm on the ground."

"Ah yes, well, that's what I forgot to tell you about the spell," Gerum replied. "The spell has a side effect. Even though it makes you powerful, it also drains your energy until you get used to the new power."

"Wow, thank you, Gerum, for those words of wisdom," Thomas said sarcastically.

"You're welcome, brother, anytime," Gerum replied, laughing. "Don't worry, brother, you're strong and adapt well. You will have mastery of your new strength in no time, just as you did with telekinesis. For now, let's rest and regain our strength. Then we will go after Doscare and finally up to the peak for Narvaria."

"Sounds like a plan, brother," Thomas answered in a tired manner and fell instantly asleep. Gerum ate another bowl of soup, then lay down to sleep too.

Two days passed, and the men slept soundly. On the third day, they awakened stiff and hungry. As they stretched, they noticed the corpse of Tremous was gone and only the bones remained.

"What happened to the corpse?" Thomas asked as Gerum rose up.

"What do you mean?" he asked and looked at the pile of bones. "I don't know. Maybe wolves or jackals. Any manner of creatures could have eaten the meat," Gerum replied.

Yes, but down to the bones? Only a dragon could eat such meat in a short amount of time, Thomas thought to himself. Then he replied, "I'm going to skin that dragon alive. Not even a troll's corpse should be desecrated in such a manner. Trust me, Gerum, I will avenge all who have been hurt by that dragon, friend or foe."

"Well, that's a good thought, brother, but we should really be going. If we stay here any longer, we may become food for the dragon next," Gerum replied.

"You're right, brother, let's go."

The two began to climb the mountain. While following a trail, they came across a small lake and meadow.

"This looks like a great spot to rest," Gerum announced with excitement.

"Yes, we have been climbing this mountain for three full days and nights. We need food and rest," Thomas answered.

"I am afraid the best meat we can find is a mountain goat or lion here," Gerum explained.

"Sounds good to me. I can cook anything, and if we can milk a goat, we can take some time to make cheese. We're in no rush, after all," Thomas explained in excitement.

"Okay, we're off on a food hunt. First one back with the most does not have to cook. Is it a deal, Thomas?"

"Yes, deal, brother. Let's go."

The two took off in opposite directions along the mountain. As Gerum traveled, he found berries, roots, rabbits, squirrels, and other small game. Thomas found three goats and some herbs. As Thomas was heading back, he noticed what he thought was a hallucination. Just in a small clearing was a woman. Thomas saw her back; he rubbed his eyes, and she disappeared.

I must be losing my mind, Thomas thought.

They both arrived at the camp at the same time.

"I win!" they both shouted.

In Gerum's defense, he claimed, "I have caught and gathered the most, so I do not have to cook."

Thomas laughed. "That was not the deal. I caught the biggest, so I do not have to cook."

"Okay," Gerum replied, "I have another bet to wager."

"I'm listening," said Thomas with great interest.

"We each get a stone, and the one who can skip it across the lake the farthest wins. Deal?"

Thomas laughed. "Deal."

With my new strength, this will be easy, Thomas thought while smiling. They each grabbed a stone and prepared to throw. Gerum started, "Ready, three, two, one, go!" and they both threw. Thomas's rock flew all the way across and through the trees. Gerum's skipped along the water and halfway through, fell in with a splash.

"Yeaaah! I win!" yelled Gerum.

"No, you did not," Thomas retorted. "I threw mine the farthest, so I won."

"Yes, you did," Gerum laughed, "but remember the rule. The one who skips the rock the farthest wins, so I won, brother."

In anger, Thomas slammed his hands on the ground and cracked it in half.

"Fine, I will cook," Thomas said in defeat.

"No, brother, we both will. Let's make a real feast because look what I have found." Gerum pulled out some wild berries and roots.

"Can that be?" Thomas looked. "Makon roots and lock berries—those make the finest wine in the kingdom," Thomas explained with a large smile.

"Alright, I'll cook the food, you make the wine, then we will eat and drink until we can't stand straight."

"Huzzah!" the two shouted as they began to make their feast. They made meat of all kinds, sheep's milk, golden wine, and fresh vegetables. It truly was a feast fit for a king. They ate, drank, and laughed until they were stumbling like wild children.

Just then, Thomas looked at the lake and saw the back of the same woman again. But when he closed his eyes and opened them, this time she was still there but facing Thomas. She was tall and slim, with long blonde hair down to her knees, eyes like sapphires that glowed in the moonlight, and the body of a goddess, with curves like an hourglass.

"Hey, you!" Thomas shouted to the woman. "Who are you?"

Gerum turned and saw the woman and shouted, "Hey, lady, come to the feast. We have food and wine fit for a beauty like yourself," just before falling over in a drunken mess.

The lady did not reply but rather seemed to dissolve into the water. *Who was that woman?* Thomas thought. *I must see her again*, as he drank down another gulp of wine and fell over just like Gerum, and they passed out drunk.

7

THE NEXT MORNING, Gerum and Thomas awoke to find all their provisions and equipment were gone. With their heads aching and their bodies limp from the late night of drinking, the two tried to piece together their foggy night.

"What happened?" Gerum asked Thomas

"I don't know. I was hoping you would tell me," Thomas answered.

"Where is all of our stuff?" Gerum asked in a daze. This question made Thomas sober up quickly and regain his senses.

"I don't know. It was all stolen, but by who?" Thomas thought to himself for a while, recalling the memory of the previous night when suddenly, "I got it! It was that woman!" shouted Thomas.

"What woman?" Gerum replied, confused and looking at Thomas in a crazy manner. "There are no women on this mountain except for Narvaria. At least that's what I have heard."

Thomas told Gerum of the beautiful woman as he remembered her in detail.

As Gerum pondered his words, he could only say one thing about this mystery woman.

"It must be Hexia, the water goddess," Gerum explained. "There's not a lot known about her except she's powerful. It's rumored she has the ability to change her form at will and has the power to charm any man or woman with an uncontrollable lust. This lust power makes the victim go mad to the point of killing others for her bidding. Legend also says that the one who is marked as her victim will see glimpses of her at first, then meet her and speak to her, then finally fall under her spell."

Thomas listened to every word with intent and caution; however, he did not believe such a being existed, so he asked, "Okay, what happens to those who become her victims?"

"She will use them as either bodyguards, or worse, she will drown them and absorb their body through the water that she controls. That would explain this lake. We must have walked into her domain by accident," Gerum said with a gloomy sigh. "It also seems like she has chosen her victim," Gerum said, looking at Thomas.

"You mean me? But if that's true, then why steal our stuff?" Thomas asked with a puzzled look on his face.

"That's easy…to separate us," Gerum answered.

"Then we just won't separate, Gerum. We will stay together and look for our things together."

"I'm afraid it is not that simple, Thomas. You see, she can move anything anywhere in her domain, but we also don't know how far her domain stretches."

"So what do you suggest?" Thomas asked.

"Let's wait. She has to return to the water at night to recover her power. When she arrives, we will spring a trap for her," Gerum replied.

"And do you have a plan for this trap, brother?"

"Of course," answered Gerum. "We will use the armor you're wearing. She may be a water goddess, and it may not capture her completely, but it can take her power and slow her down to the point we can capture her," Gerum explained with a smile.

"Okay, but how do you capture water?" asked Thomas.

"Simple, brother, with the bottles we used for the wine, we can trap her in them and make her tell us where our equipment is."

"I like it," Thomas replied with a grin.

"But be warned, brother." Gerum stopped smiling. "Only you can see her because you're her victim. I won't be able to help you until you have weakened her power enough for me to see and aid in capturing her, so you will be on your own. You will have to meet her and act as her pawn, but do not succumb to her. Remember, she can see your inner desires and use them against you."

"Okay, brother. If I feel like I'm losing control, I will run back here as fast as I can."

"Okay, brother, be careful. I will be here setting the trap."

After this, Thomas and Gerum spent the whole day planning the trap. When the sun set, Gerum lay in wait, and Thomas sat by the lakeside. Suddenly, the voice of a true angel said, "Excuse me, sir, are you alone?"

As Thomas turned around, he was captivated by a beautiful, voluptuous woman standing in nothing more than a white cloth. Thomas's heart began to beat rapidly in his chest as he stuttered, "Y-y-yes, my name is Thomas. I'm here just taking in the scene and resting."

"I see. My name is Hexia. I live on this mountain and don't get a lot of visitors around here." Her voice had Thomas hanging on every word. "May I ask why you're traveling through here? Are you after the golden dragon on the peak of the mountain?"

This comment made Thomas snap out of his trance. "I'm going to kill her and claim all her scales to bring the land prosperity for an eternity and avenge all those who foolishly worshipped the false golden dragon. Gerum, now!" Thomas yelled.

Gerum ran out quickly and attempted to speak the magic spell to trap Hexia. However, she read Thomas's mind and knew he was there.

"I have something for you, welp!" she screamed and threw a water ball that covered Gerum's mouth in water so he couldn't speak properly. "And just for defying me, here's yours!" She leaned over and kissed Thomas passionately. Thomas began to go limp, and his eyes turned red as he looked at Gerum. "Now, my darling, kill him!" Hexia commanded Thomas.

Thomas, with no words, began walking over to Gerum and, using his telekinesis, pinned Gerum to a tree. Gerum, now free from the water, yelled, "Ha kai sektop!" This made Thomas feel woozy but slowed him down. Gerum then quickly recited the incantation, and Thomas's armor began to shine blue.

Hexia noticed her power draining fast and began to panic and headed toward the water. Thomas, now regaining his senses, screamed out, "Oh no, you don't!" and grabbed the water goddess by the legs. She tried desperately to turn her legs to water and slip through Thomas's grasp, but it was no good. With her power draining, she was becoming more solid and more childlike.

Finally, after she stopped struggling, she reverted to her true form, a small little girl who looked no more than eight years old. "Let me go, you brute," she yelled as Thomas quickly threw her next to Gerum and said, "You're not a woman. You're a little girl."

Gerum used nearby vines to create ropes and bind Hexia. "Where's our stuff, Hexia?" Thomas demanded.

"If you must know, it is in the lake, but you can't reach it as the lake is my power. If you let me go, I will kill you both."

This made Gerum angry, and he hit her on the head. "Don't think just because you're a little girl now it does not mean we won't beat the stuffing out of you. Now tell us how we get it all back," Gerum demanded in anger.

"Just jump in and get it. It is only water, after all," Hexia explained.

Thomas, without thinking, jumped into the lake and began to swim.

"Oh, did I forget to mention the lake bottom is one hundred miles down? He will die trying," Hexia explained, laughing at Thomas's plight.

Gerum, now angry and worried, looked out for Thomas, only to see no Thomas surfacing. "Thomas!" Gerum yelled. No answer.

Hexia began to laugh. "He is dead. Oh well, I kind of liked him. I would have made him a good slave, then eaten him. He would have lived a glorious life worshipping me. Oh well."

Gerum, in anger, grabbed Hexia and bound her to a nearby tree. "There, now you can't move without me," Gerum replied, smiling. He began to run off, leaving Hexia screaming and writhing in anger. Suddenly, a loud splash was heard, and Thomas came crawling out of the lake, coughing up water.

"Thomas, are you all right?" Gerum asked, worried.

"Yes, brother, I am okay, but it is so far down I can't get anything."

"Why not use your telekinesis, brother?" Gerum offered.

"Yea, let's try that. Where's Hexia?" Thomas asked, and as if almost on cue, Hexia leaped over the duo with vines in her mouth and dived deep into the water. Suddenly, loud laughter was heard, and the water began to twist and turn, creating a giant blue-colored water monster. Ten feet tall, with tentacles everywhere, glowing yellow eyes, and breasts the size of mountains, Hexia screamed, "Now, you mortals, die!" as she threw a massive water tentacle at Thomas and Gerum.

8

"Move!" shouted Thomas as they barely dodged the flying tentacle. Thomas unsheathed his sword and prepared for battle while Gerum retreated to the forest to come up with a plan. Suddenly, another two massive tentacles came after Thomas. One tried to pierce him while the other attempted to grab him. Thomas, in a frantic act, attempted to cut the tentacles only to discover they were made of water.

"Oh no!" Thomas yelled as the tentacles grabbed him and lifted him into the air.

"You can't harm me, mortal. I'm made of water—you can't cut me!" Hexia boasted.

Suddenly, Gerum ran out of the forest. "Thomas, that's it!" he shouted.

As Thomas struggled to breathe under the crushing weight of the tentacles, he replied, "What's it? You got a plan, brother?"

"Of course! She's made of water, and you absorbed her power. That means, to some degree, you also have control over water. Come on, Thomas, concentrate—you can break out!"

Thomas then closed his eyes and felt the power rumble to life within the armor. Suddenly, a blue wave washed over him, and his whole body became covered in a blue aura. He then let the tentacles consume him and opened his hands wide, destroying the tentacles using the power he absorbed from Hexia.

With a loud scream, Hexia's tentacles fell off her monstrous body and landed back into the soil. Thomas then fell to the ground, and Hexia reached for Gerum with her tentacles, screaming, "I'll kill you, mortal! Shut your mouth!"

Gerum yelled, "Thomas, look! The water around our stuff is gone now. Quickly, I'll distract her. You get the stuff!"

Without words, Thomas ran for their equipment, and Gerum began taunting Hexia. "Hey, Hexia! You're some goddess to be fooled by some dumb mortals. You can't—ooowwwww!"

Hexia grabbed Gerum in an attempt to drown him. "I'll swallow you whole and drown you and absorb all your mortal essence!" She quickly threw Gerum down her monstrous mouth, but Gerum just smiled and revealed a hammer and a bag. He struck the bag, and a loud boom of an explosion was heard.

As Thomas grabbed their stuff, he looked up, only to see Gerum go flying. Then Thomas was slammed by hundreds of gallons of water, barreling him into the ground. Thomas quickly got out of the hole and rushed to Gerum.

In a daze, Gerum heard Thomas screaming, "Gerum! Gerum! Wake up, Gerum!"

Gerum sat up, eyes blurry and in a haze. As he saw Thomas, he shouted, "Thomas! Over here!"

Thomas met Gerum in concern and asked, "Are you alright? What was that?"

Gerum replied, "I've been better. Pressure powder—I use it to stress test armor when it's completed. It makes a big bang but also causes a lot of damage."

"And how much did you use on Hexia, brother?" Thomas asked.

"All of it," Gerum said, laughing.

"I think that explosion made you crazy, brother. I'll bet Hexia is down for the count after that one!" Thomas exclaimed in reverence for Gerum's bravery.

"Don't count on it. She's a water goddess. It may have stunned her, but I feel she's far from dead or even defeated for that matter."

Just then, the earth began to shake, and all the nearby forest dried up and died instantly.

In the hole where Hexia once was now stood a gigantic, twenty-foot-tall monstrous womanlike creature with angel-like wings. Everything from her hair and wings to her breasts and feet was made entirely of mud and clay. The earth around her began to shake as the water goddess yelled, "You mortals have gone too far. This ends now," and began to hover in the air, ready for battle.

"Gerum, you have done enough, brother. Let me beat this new version of Hexia," Thomas said.

"Be careful," Gerum explained. "She may be more solid now and can be harmed, but she's ten times more powerful. Your control over water will not be as effective this time around. Use your head, Thomas," Gerum says in a concerned manner.

"Don't worry, brother. I will expose her weakness, and this time, we will kill her and take all her power." Thomas then leaped away from Gerum and readied himself for battle.

Hexia, without words, began to spin in midair and launched feather-shaped clay that looked like arrows at Thomas with lightning speed.

Thomas began to run, only to find he couldn't match Hexia's speed. He was quickly hit by the feathers, launching him over ten feet back.

You're strong, Thomas thought to himself. *Let's see how you manage this.* Thomas then used his super strength to pick up a nearby boulder and launch it at Hexia, only to have her smash the boulder with her fist. This attack managed to damage Hexia, though, as her hand exploded into pieces.

Thomas, with a smile, said, "Ha! You can be hurt in this form. Then try this." He then grabbed a handful of stones and began to throw them like mini rockets. Each one pierced the clay body of Hexia, and she screamed in anger and frustration.

"You're getting on my nerves, mortal," Hexia said. She then healed herself as the holes in her body and her hand returned to normal in an instant. She threw her fists, and they detached like two giant missiles aimed right at Thomas.

Thomas grabbed his sword and slashed directly in the direction of the two giant mounds of mud and clay, cutting them back in two. They barely missed him. This, however, left Thomas greatly weakened.

I have to find her weak point and end this soon, Thomas thought to himself.

As Thomas was lost in his thoughts, thinking of a plan to defeat Hexia, she pulled out another surprise. She shrank down to the size of an average woman, looking like a mud angel, then split herself into four other clones and circled Thomas.

"Let's see how you handle this, mortal," she taunted.

Suddenly, Hexia and the clones moved toward Thomas so fast he had no choice but to jump in the air. Two of the clones followed him and began swinging punches and kicks at him.

If they moved only a hair faster, I would be in big trouble, Thomas thought. *Good thing I can counter.* Thomas began to swing his sword to block the two clones and noticed a surprising phenomenon. *Wow, these clones are dry and only have minimal water in them. I'll bet I can cut them down and absorb their water into the armor, but I need to remember the spell.*

Suddenly, with a thought, Thomas remembered the spell, and without speaking, the spell activated and absorbed all the water in the clones. *Ha, I can activate it with my mind. Wait, that's it! I can use the clones against Hexia! Let's see how she likes this.*

Just then, Thomas used his telekinesis to make the now-dry clones stop attacking and face Hexia. He launched the clones at the third and fourth clones of the water goddess. With a loud bang, the clones slammed into one another and turned to dust.

Hexia, now alone again, grimaced. *Damn, this mortal is strong! This is using up a lot of my power, and I'm running low on strength. Wait, I have an idea, but it will be a risk,* she thought.

Dazed in her thoughts, she forgot Thomas was on the attack. As she looked up, he yelled, "Die!" and slashed her body in two.

Ah, I was careless! I have to flee, thought Hexia as she turned into water and fled the crumbling second form.

Thomas put down his sword and ran to Gerum, who was still unconscious from the explosion earlier. "Gerum, Gerum, wake up! She's gone, Gerum."

"I'm awake, but why are you whispering?" Gerum shouted, only realizing his hearing took a temporary blow. "I can't hear you well."

Thomas yelled back, "She's gone! We won!"

"Great, let's collect our stuff."

As the two returned to the now crater that was once the lake, they noticed a woman naked by the side. "Who is that?" Gerum yelled.

It's Hexia, thought Thomas. He grabbed his sword and prepared for battle once again, but this time, Hexia looked at Thomas with alluring eyes and spoke, "I give up. You win. I surrender to you. I will be your slave, and you can use me any way you like."

Thomas looked at her defiantly and responded, "How can I trust you? You just tried to kill us and steal all of our equipment. I should kill you rather than trust you."

"Then kill me. I'm done. But before you do, I have one request," Hexia said lovingly.

"And what is that?" said Thomas.

"Kiss me. Kiss me as if I'm a lover, and you can freely kill me afterwards. That's all I ask."

"Why?" Thomas asked in disbelief.

"Because I have never been beaten before, and now that I have, I want to experience real love's kiss before I die. That's all I ask."

Gerum shouted, "Don't do it. It's a trap, Thomas! She only wants to stab you in the back. Don't believe it."

Before Gerum could convince Thomas, he took Hexia in his arms and kissed her passionately. Sparks instantly flew between the two as if they were a married couple deeply in love. Suddenly, Hexia's blue eyes turned red, and she grabbed the back of Thomas's head.

She's going to drain his life force! I need to do something, but I am too weak, thought Gerum.

Just then, Thomas grabbed her head, and a blue aura formed around him. In an instant, Hexia was reduced back to her true form, and her red eyes became white and shallow. Thomas had absorbed all the remaining water power Hexia possessed and left her unconscious.

"Let's kill her!" shouted Gerum as he grabbed a dagger from his back.

"No, we need to wake her up." Thomas then took some water from a puddle in the ground and poured it over Hexia.

She sprang back to life. "What the hell was that!" she screamed, only to realize she had no power anymore.

"I absorbed and stole your power. If you want it back, you will have to earn it," Thomas bluffed, as he did not know how to give it back.

"And how will I do that?" Hexia yelled.

"By serving me," Thomas explained with a menacing grin and laugh. "I have big plans for you."

"You're not going to fuck a child, are you? I'll kill myself before I become anyone's sex slave!"

"What? No! You're going to be my maid and serve me in the battles ahead."

"And if I don't?"

"Then I will kill you here, and Gerum and I will obtain the golden dragon's power for ourselves."

The golden dragon's power? With that, I could double or even triple my powers. Then I could kill these mortals, she thought carefully. "Okay then, I accept your offer, but only to further my own needs," Hexia explained.

"Don't forget, I have your power, and you are going to help me control it on our journey. Understand?"

"What? No. I'm not going to allow you to use my powers against me. That's just cruel, mortal."

"My name is Thomas, and it's either that, or we leave you here with that muddy puddle full of shit water I used to revive you," Thomas said, laughing.

Hexia puked. "Fine, anything is better than this. By the way, there is your stuff in the hole. Go get it, and we can get going."

"No problem," Thomas said as he faced the crater and yelled, "Rise and come to me!"

Just then, all their equipment rose out of the crater and hovered over to the trio. "Right, let's get our gear together and get going."

Gerum shouted, "Oh, I have missed you!" and kissed his equipment with the same love Thomas kissed Hexia with. The other two turned their heads in disgust.

"Here, Hexia, you can have this," Thomas said as he made her a travel backpack just like his but smaller and holding bags of water. This was the first time someone had done anything kind for Hexia in two hundred years. She looked at Thomas with tears in her eyes. She said, "Thank you."

Two hundred years ago, Hexia married a mortal who found her severely dehydrated and nursed her back to health. Even though she was a goddess, she could never bear children. But the mortal man loved her anyways, and for forty years after that, Hexia was happy and in love. When he died, so did her heart, and from then on, she used her looks to make herself more powerful.

Today, Thomas, in not so many ways, did the same thing her husband did all those years ago. Hexia, for the first time in two hundred years, felt her heart beating once again.

"Thank you, Thomas. I will follow you, and I will train you. For your kindness, I will also defend you," she said. *For you have rekindled my love for humans, and the fire of my love for you has been ignited,* she thought, not daring to say that last part out loud due to embarrassment.

As the new team began to set off, Hexia looked at Thomas with great affection.

"What are you looking at?" Thomas asked in a confused manner.

"Nothing, just excited to help you, that's all," she replied.

Huh, just a day ago she was trying to kill us, and now it seems as though she's like a lovestruck schoolgirl. Women are so complicated, Thomas thought to himself.

Gerum said nothing as the three walked into a forest clearing and began to make camp for the night.

"Let's camp here. Gerum, you and I can make the fire and hunt something good to eat. Hexia, you're getting us fresh water," Thomas laid out all the rules.

Hexia retorted, "Why don't you and I go get fresh water and Gerum set up camp?"

"No, that would not be fair. Besides, Gerum knows how to give you your powers back. You don't want to offend him, do you?" Thomas explained, looking at Hexia with a grin.

Gerum interjected, "Why don't we make Hexia set up camp and get us water? After all, she did try to kill us." He laughed hysterically the whole time.

Hexia lashed out in anger, "Oh, youuu! Fine. I'll go fetch the water. I swear all men are the same," and she stormed off to find water.

As Gerum and Thomas set up camp, Gerum looked to Thomas. "Are you sure it is safe to bring her along, Thomas?" he asked with concern.

"Do not worry, brother. I'm more powerful than her thanks to you. She's no threat as long as we have her full water power in the armor."

"Okay." Gerum sighed in relief. "I can't go deaf twice, you know." Gerum laughed as he said this.

"By the way, how are your injuries, brother?" Thomas asked with concern, remembering.

"They will heal. I only suffered the concussion of the blast. Hexia got the most, at least her water body did."

"By the way, how did you make that bomb? It was genius," Thomas asked, looking excited and curious.

"Ah, my dear brother, it was pressure powder."

"Pressure powder?" Thomas looked confused. "What is pressure powder?"

"Oh yes, I forgot. You don't smith, so you couldn't know about it. Pressure powder is made from a stone high on this mountain. The stone can be ground into a powder form, and when the powder is struck hard, it gives off tremendous force."

"Gerum, that's amazing!" he said, taking in all the new information.

"Yes, well, unfortunately, we're all out. I used what I had on Hexia to immobilize her," Gerum explained with a sigh.

"Well, if it is on this mountain, let's just go get some. Where do we go?" Thomas asked in excitement.

"I'm sorry, brother, it is not that easy. Now ever since Doscare decided to use the stones for his magic, he's turned away smiths or those who gave him attitude or offended him. He would either blow them up or use them for his experiments with his magic."

"What kind of magic power does he have?" Thomas asked.

"All kinds. He has telekinesis, elemental magic, confusion magic—really any magic you can think of. Plus, he is not like the other trolls. He is handsome, tall, and looks more human than a troll. The only way you can know he is a troll is the two horns protruding from his long brown hair. He also has glowing red eyes and a smile more beautiful than the most handsome man in the world. His muscular body is ridged with muscle like his brother's, but his tan skin mimics a human. He also wears a striped suit and always has a bone in his teeth like a toothpick."

"Thank you for the description, brother, but if you know so much about Doscare, I'm assuming you went to see him?"

"Yes, I did. It was two years ago, before I made your armor. I went to him and asked for some pressure powder. I bowed my head in respect, and he liked this, so he gave me the bag I had. It was a lot for a smith, but he sat back down on a throne of pressure powder stone as if it was nothing."

"So what you're saying is as long as we are nice to him and respectful, he should let us pass without a fight?" Thomas asked.

"I don't think so. Even though you can get pressure powder from him, I have never heard of anyone going past him, at least no one alive, that is," Gerum explained.

"How far is he from here?" Thomas asked in a curious tone.

"We're almost halfway up the mountain now, so he shouldn't be far. Ah, the fire's done. Let's get some meat and vegetables on this fire, and we can eat soon," Gerum said.

"Sounds good to me. I'm starving," Thomas said, licking his lips.

About this time, Hexia returned with two giant barrels full of water.

"Wow, you really are the water goddess," Thomas stated in excitement. "That's enough water to last the whole trip!"

Gerum looked and said in surprise, "Well, when you're good, you're good."

"Thank you," said Hexia, gloating. "What smells so amazing?" she asked.

"Oh, we're roasting a wild boar we caught and some vegetables," Thomas explained.

Hexia's stomach growled loudly, so loud that Thomas and Gerum could hear. "Do you want some? I did not know goddesses needed to eat," Thomas said.

"We don't normally, but you have my power, so I am mortal for now. Thanks to you, I have to eat and sleep just like a human. However, I can teach you a trick to make this boar better."

"How is that?" Thomas asked, drooling at the thought.

"Take some of this water and use my power to soak the boar from the inside out. This will be your first lesson," she said. "Now raise your right hand and think about the water penetrating the meat and circulating all through it," Hexia explained in detail, and Thomas listened attentively.

Then he raised his right hand, and the water from one of the barrels began to rise and flow into the boar's hide. The steam created a cloud of aroma in the air that made all three of them drool uncontrollably. Thomas concentrated and could see the water flowing into the meat and through the body of the boar before vaporizing into the air. "I can see it," Thomas explained in excitement

"Yes, but do not lose focus or it won't come out right."

After a few minutes of doing this, the leg of the boar fell off and into the fire.

"Stop! It's done!" Hexia yelled in admiration.

Gerum quickly moved the boar off the fire and onto some leaves they had made for plates. The boar fell completely apart, and steam burst forth in a cloud of succulence.

"This is amazing!" Thomas and Gerum said in unison.

"This is steamed boar. The meat falls right off the bone," Hexia replied.

The new team ate the whole boar and all the vegetables in a flash, and with their bellies full, they lay down to rest.

As the night was quiet, Thomas looked over at Hexia and asked, "Hexia, what do you know about Doscare?"

Hexia instantly sat up. "Excuse me, did you just say Doscare?" she asked in a sudden angry tone.

"Yes, I asked Gerum about him, and he told me a little, but I want to know what you know."

"He's an arrogant ass. We had a relationship for a few years, but he was so absorbed with himself and not me that it made me sick. He was kind and charming until that bastard dragon came to see him and gave him the power to change his looks."

"You mean Narvaria, right?" Thomas asked.

"No. The black dragon Zerok. He showed up two years ago and offered him the power to rule the mountain, and he offered me dominion over all water, even off the mountain." Hexia continued, "I said no way, but Doscare instantly said yes. He hated his appearance, but I liked him for his heart. He was always obsessed with magic, but he also used it to please me and keep me happy. After that day, he focused only on himself and his magic, and I was cast out of his life. If I get the chance, I'll kill him. I promise that, Thomas," Hexia said as tears appeared in her eyes.

"I'm sorry, Hexia. I did not mean to upset you," Thomas said, full of remorse.

"It's okay, Thomas. You didn't know. I just get so emotional thinking about it. That's why I attacked people, because they only cared to see the outside of me, not this form of me or my heart."

Gripped by emotion, Thomas grabbed Hexia and hugged her tightly. "I see you, Hexia, and you will always be a good friend."

Hexia could not control it anymore, and her tears flowed like a river. After a little while, Thomas said, "Let's get some sleep okay? Tomorrow, we will find Doscare, and we will kill him together. What do you say?"

Hexia nodded in silence and lay down to sleep.

"Oh, I forgot!" Hexia jumped up in excitement. "Thomas, give me your hand. I want to give you something."

"Um, okay." Thomas gave Hexia his right hand. Hexia chanted some magic words, and a bright blue symbol appeared on the back of Thomas's hand.

"What is this?" Thomas asked.

"It's my goddess symbol. With it, you can command the water with your mind with ease. Consider it a gift for the way I treated you two. Tomorrow I will also teach you how to use water as a weapon."

Thomas in excitement nodded, and they both lay back down to sleep.

"Wake up, sleepyhead." Hexia stroked Thomas's beard to wake him up. *He's so cute when he's sleeping*, Hexia thought as a loud fart came from Gerum. *He's gross even while sleeping.*

Suddenly, Thomas woke up with a loud grunt.

"Good morning," Hexia said happily. "Today I'm going to teach you how to control the water element you have, and by the way, just to be clear, you did not steal my power."

"What do you mean? You mean you have your power back?" Thomas questioned.

"No, not fully. That will take some time, but yes, I can regenerate my power as long as there's water around."

Great, then she will be a threat again, Thomas thought.

Hexia quickly retorted, "And I won't be a threat. You beat me, so I'll follow you. Deal?"

"What? How did you…?" Thomas looked at Hexia in confusion.

"Mind-reading power. I am a goddess, after all. Now let's get some food and eat, then we will begin your training."

At that moment, Gerum let out a loud burp, still sleeping.

Ugh, Thomas thought, *at least he's a good smith. If he didn't have that, he would be the grossest in town.*

About that time, Hexia burst into laughter.

Stop reading my mind, thought Thomas.

Okay, fine, she replied to Thomas in his mind.

When they returned from gathering fruits and vegetables, Gerum was awake and making a fire. They sat down and began to eat.

"Did everyone sleep okay?" asked Gerum.

"I slept alright," said Thomas.

"I don't sleep. I lay down and just circulate my power to rejuvenate my body. We both know you slept well," said Hexia, laughing.

As Gerum took a spoonful of food, he looked up, confused, and asked, "How do you know that?"

Thomas, laughing said, "Your belly told us this morning."

Still confused, Gerum just shrugged. "So what are we doing today?" he asked.

Thomas thought for a minute and said, "Well, we've been on a long journey already, and we need to really resupply. So today, let's look for meat we can smoke. The more, the better. We can dry it out and eat it along the way so that it doesn't spoil. Then we can grab a lot of fruits and vegetables we find to take with us, and finally, a fresh full supply of water. If we can restock what we lost, we will not be concerned with running out of food and water."

Hexia responded, "Sounds good to me, but if we restock today, when am I going to train you, Thomas?"

"You can train me tomorrow. We will take a few days here since it seems food is plentiful on this side of the mountain. We can rest for a while, and I can get a good grip on using all my new powers," he replied.

"That is a great idea, and I can take my time and reinforce your armor and your weapon while we're here. We can even make this our halfway base as I believe we're not far from the peak of the mountain," Gerum stated.

"Okay, let's finish eating, then get to it first. Gerum and I will find meat. You find fruits and vegetables, Hexia."

"Yeah, yeah, I got it. Don't worry," Hexia replied.

Soon after they finished, they all set out for the day.

After several hours, they returned with a great deal in tow. Thomas came back with four bucks, three does, an elk, and two mountain lions. Gerum returned with twelve rabbits, ten squirrels, eight raccoons, and four ferrets. Hexia returned with twenty sacks of assorted roots, cabbage, squash, apples, carrots, lettuce, cucumbers, onions, and corn.

They all sat down and were amazed at everyone else's gatherings. As Gerum and Thomas began skinning and cooking the meat, Hexia cut up some fruits and vegetables and made a delicious meat stew. The three ate until they were about to burst.

As Thomas and Gerum fell fast asleep, Hexia used her power to create a water barrier around their camp to prevent other animals from stealing their smoking meat. As she circulated her power, she couldn't help but feel a dark and ominous presence coming from Gerum. *I don't know what it is, but something is not right about Gerum.*

Hexia then released a small amount of water that went up Gerum's pointed nose and down into his body. Using her power, she circulated the drop through his body until the water suddenly became vaporized and a burn mark appeared on Hexia's hand. She winced in pain. *He has dark power in him.*

The next morning, Gerum and Thomas awoke to notice the barrier.

"Did you protect us all night, Hexia?" Thomas asked.

"Of course, I was not about to let enemies steal our food."

"Oh, is that the only reason?" Gerum teased. Hexia then threw a water ball at Gerum, soaking him. Gerum looked at Hexia and stared with a "that's not funny" look. This had Hexia and Thomas rolling with laughter, but she quickly stopped laughing and looked at Gerum with killing intent.

"Hey, what's that look for?" Gerum asked, turning his head.

"Oh, it's nothing," Hexia replied as she got up and looked at Thomas. "It is time for your training, Thomas. Let's go." She grabbed Thomas and dragged him off into the forest.

What's her problem? Gerum thought as he wrung out his wet clothes and lay back down to bask in the sun.

Hexia led Thomas into the woods, thick with trees. "Okay, first know that water is like emotion. If you can control your emotion, you can control the water easily. If you can't, you won't. Simple."

"Okay, so what emotions are used?" asked Thomas.

"The emotion you possess that is the most powerful. For example, mine used to be love—the willingness to protect—but now for me, it's drive and determination. So think of an emotion that drives you."

Thomas closed his eyes and thought of his father and the golden dragon. Anger and sadness sprung forth. This caused the armor to glow blue.

"That's it," Hexia replied. "Now remember, water is, well, water. It can be made into any weapon you think of. So let's try something simple. Let's make a ball. Think about a ball and use your emotion to craft it."

Thomas thought about a ball and threw it at the golden dragon. A huge ball of water, the size of a boulder, appeared in Thomas's hand.

"Wow, what power!" Hexia was amazed at the size of the ball. *And on his first try, too. He's a natural*, Hexia thought in excitement.

Just then, Thomas opened his eyes and saw the water ball. *Wow, what a huge…* His thoughts quickly changed as the ball lost its form and splashed everywhere. Thomas lost consciousness and blacked out.

Ugh. Hexia looked at Thomas. *He used all his power in one go. Go figure.*

A few minutes later, Thomas awoke and looked at Hexia. "What happened?" he asked.

"You blacked out. You used too much power."

"So how do we prevent that?" Thomas asked.

"Easy. We take it slow. First, let's try making a small ball. But this time, don't concentrate so hard. Just relax, be like the water, and let your emotion form the ball."

This time, Thomas created a much smaller ball and did not black out. "Wow, I can feel it!" Thomas exclaimed with excitement.

"Okay, good. Now try releasing the ball at that tree."

"Just look at the tree and throw like a rock?" Thomas asked.

"Exactly."

Thomas then put his arm back and threw the ball. It smashed against the tree with a splash.

"Okay, good. Now we're going to practice this for a little while, okay?" Hexia explained. "After that, we will weaponize it."

After a few hours, Thomas could make a ball without even thinking and throw it without using his arm.

"This is boring now, Hexia," Thomas began to complain. "Let's do something else."

Hexia gave in to the whining Thomas. "Let's try this." She made a giant axe out of water and slashed down four trees.

"Wow, that's amazing!" Thomas looked in surprise.

"Now you think about making a weapon, give it more form, and cut down these trees," Hexia explained.

Thomas thought, and a flurry of water spikes appeared. Just then, Thomas yelled, "Go!" and put his arms forward. At least one hundred spikes sliced through the trees as if they were paper.

"That was awesome, Hexia, but now I'm dizzy," Thomas said as he fell down and sat in one place. "My head hurts," he told her with concern.

"It's okay, Thomas. The more power you use, the more your body has to get used to it. Take your time. We're in no rush here," Hexia explained.

"You're right. Let's go back and check on Gerum," he said.

"Okay, Thomas, let's go."

Thomas got up, and they headed back to camp.

Upon arriving, they noticed Gerum with a bright red sunburn all over his body. He had fallen asleep in the sun while waiting for his clothes to dry.

"Oooowww!" Gerum woke up screaming. "I'm on fire!" He jumped up and started running all around the camp, causing Hexia and Thomas to burst into hysterical laughter.

"You're not on fire, dummy," Hexia taunted. "You're sunburned. You were in the sun too long. Hold still."

Hexia then shot a stream of water around Gerum, both cooling and healing his burnt body.

"Aaahhhhhhh," Gerum sighed in relief. "That's much better. Thank you, Hexia."

Hexia just turned her body and grabbed a bowl of food. After eating, the trio stayed awake and watched the stars.

"You know, when we find the golden dragon and I kill her, maybe my armor can absorb power from her. Maybe I can make everyone in the town have good fortune forever," Thomas said.

"Is that why you're going up there? You do know Narvaria is guarded by a master swordsman, right?" Hexia said, bewildered.

Gerum and Thomas both sat up and looked at Hexia.

"Yeah, a master swordsman. She saved his life, and now he's immortal and guards her fearlessly. He's never been beaten. Even Doscare has lost to him."

"And this swordsman's name is what?" Thomas questioned.

"I don't know. All I know is if you want to get to Narvaria, you will have to kill an immortal sword master. You two up for that?"

Thomas looked at Gerum. "Did you know about this, brother?" Thomas asked with concern.

"Honestly, I did not know. This is new to me. But, Thomas, can you beat someone like that?" Gerum said.

"I don't know," said Thomas.

"You can't," Hexia interrupted. "The only way you can win is by having a sword made of dragon bone, tempered in dragon fire, and blessed by a goddess. That's the only way you can injure the immortal."

10

"WELL, WE GOT one of those," Gerum replied and looked at Hexia. "You can bless the weapon, right?"

"Of course, but to bless a weapon, I would have to imprint my own goddess power into it, and I am nowhere near powerful enough to do that now," she explained.

"Okay, well, we don't have a dragon bone sword or dragon fire either," Thomas retorted.

"Um, excuse me, we can create dragon flame," Gerum stated in an excited manner. "Remember the pressure powder from the stones Doscare hoards? Well, combining flame with pressure powder and some other ingredients creates white fire, also known as dragon's fire, so if we had a dragon's bone I could forge you a mighty sword."

"Okay, but how are we going to find a dragon bone?" Hexia retorted with sarcasm.

The three fell silent and continued to look up at the sky until the two men fell asleep.

During the night, Hexia watched as she always did, but suddenly, out of nowhere, she found she was tired, and circulating her power was not working, and she fell asleep.

The next morning, she woke to Thomas smiling above her. "So I guess you do sleep, after all," Thomas ridiculed her in a teasing manner.

"I don't know what happened. I was fine, then I got tired, and next thing I know, I'm waking up to your ugly face," she replied, teasing him right back.

"Where's Gerum?" she asked.

"I don't know. He was gone before I woke up."

Just then, a shout came from the nearby woods. "Yeeahhh! I found it!" yelled Gerum.

Thomas and Hexia got up and raced to the sound of his cheering, only to find him standing beside a huge dragon tooth.

"How and where did this come from?" Thomas asked in surprise.

"Wow, it's huge," Hexia stated in shock.

"I found it this morning. I got up and thought I would go for a walk to stretch my legs and discovered it. With this, we can make the dragon blade for you, Thomas," Gerum stated excitedly.

"Okay, but two problems. One, how are we going to carry it? And two, we still need the pressure powder."

"Not to worry, Thomas. I can cut off a chunk of the tooth and use that for the sword. And we can get the pressure powder. With Hexia by our side, we can't lose."

"Alright then." Thomas swung his sword, and it cut deep into the dragon tooth. Using his super strength, he pried off a giant chunk of the tooth that Gerum quickly tied to his gear.

"This is perfect. Well done, Thomas."

"Thank you, brother. Now let's go get our powder."

The three returned to camp, packed up, and prepared to march off to find Doscare and retrieve the now precious pressure stones.

As they traveled up the mountain, Hexia asked Gerum, "Just curious, but how many pressure stones are you going to need for this sword?"

Gerum thought for a minute and replied, "At least ten large stones."

"What! Ten large stones?" Hexia replied in shock. "Doscare will not let us leave alive with ten large stones, Gerum."

"That's why we're going to kill him," interrupted Thomas.

"Oh, I see." She sighed. "Well, this is going to be fun," she replied sarcastically.

Suddenly, the smell of dust and fire reached the noses of the trio. "We're close." Everyone prepared for battle and stopped to make camp.

"We will camp here for tonight," Thomas began, but he was suddenly cut off by a bright light beam almost slamming into him.

"Excuse me." Doscare looked down, hovering over them. "Can I ask why you're here and in my territory uninvited? What do you want?"

"Doscare, my name is Thomas—"

"And I don't care," Doscare cut him off again. "All I want to know is why you're here and what you want."

"We want ten large pressure stones, and we will leave you to live," Gerum replied confidently.

You idiot, both Hexia and Thomas thought the same thing.

"Oh, really? Let me live? Well, I say no, and you're welcome to try." Suddenly, Doscare raised his arms, and the three were lifted into the air and thrown twenty feet back.

Wow, what amazing power, Thomas thought, using his telekinesis. Hexia, using her water, bound Doscare, and Thomas threw huge pressure stones at him.

"Ha! You think this is going to work?" Doscare raised his arms only to find Gerum had thrown a fire stick also. *Oh no*, he thought as he widened his fingers and created a shield. The explosion was huge and loud.

Sadly, once the smoke cleared, Doscare appeared in an orb of magic. "Is that all you got?" he shouted as he sent a powerful blast of white magic at the team.

"Move!" Thomas shouted as the white magic slammed into the ground, leaving a crater.

"You can't win," Doscare shouted menacingly. With a wave of his hands, hundreds of white orbs appeared. Hexia quickly dumped a barrel of water and turned into the first monster form Thomas and Gerum fought. Her tentacles blocked most of the orbs as Hexia and Doscare fought in midair, Doscare throwing orbs and Hexia using her tentacles like whips to block and attack.

"We have to help her!" Thomas yelled.

"Here, Thomas." Gerum ran up to Thomas and, using oil and stones, ignited Thomas's sword. "Now use your telekinesis to fight in the air."

Thomas, without a word, sent his sword flying at Doscare, and it began striking Doscare's shield repeatedly. With Hexia and Thomas fighting together, Gerum began cutting chunks of pressure stones like a madman. As the shield began to crack, Doscare shouted a magical incantation, and his shield dissipated. He drew a long sword infused with white magic and began to fight Thomas's sword.

In light of the distraction, Hexia turned into her second form, attempting to drown Doscare, only to find she could not move. As she looked up at Doscare, she quickly realized her fate.

"Oh no, I'm trapped!" she screamed. The shield Doscare used had ensnared Hexia, immobilizing her. Quickly, she sent a link message to Thomas: *Thomas, I am trapped. I can't move. Use all your powers together to overwhelm Doscare. You can do it!*

Thomas, suddenly hearing Hexia's voice, lost control, and his sword was cut in two by Doscare.

"I have had enough of these game! Die!" Doscare yelled as he put both of his hands in the air and turned into three clones. Then those clones created thousands of white condensed orbs of magical power. One orb could make a crater in the earth, and the amount he now commanded was enough to destroy the whole kingdom. It was all headed right at the team.

Thomas mustered all his strength and, using his telekinesis and water power, lifted enough pressure stones and water spikes to match Doscare blow for blow. He turned all his internal strength to his mental power, and without warning, a carnival of explosions went flying through the air. Both Doscare and Thomas were giving it their all. Doscare's left clone was blown away, but so was Gerum. Shortly after that, his second clone was blown away, and his onslaught stopped. Both Thomas and Doscare were exhausted. Doscare's eyes lit up with white magic as he yelled, "This is the end, fool! Take this!" He puts his hands together, and a monstrous beam of white light blasted at Thomas faster than lightning.

Thomas closed his eyes and thought of his father and Narvaria. His anger raged, and his whole body was engulfed with blue light. Hexia noticed this and screamed in fear, "No, Thomas, don't!"

Without another word, Thomas put his hands together, and a gigantic water and ice dragon blasted from his hands. The dragon roared as it collided with Doscare's magic beam. The two were at a stalemate. Doscare began to bleed from his eyes and ears as Thomas bled from his nose and mouth. Neither wavered an inch.

Oh no, he's dying! Hexia thought to herself as she used all her strength, broke free from the orb, and quickly flew to Thomas's aid. Hexia, in her goddess form, put her hands together and sent another monstrous water and ice dragon. The two dragons merged and formed a two-headed flying dragon that slammed into Doscare's beam, easily overpowering it. He created a shield to quickly guard himself, only to have it smash him into the pressure stones. In a fury of explosions, the shield shattered, and Doscare was blasted from the front and bombed from the back. When the smoke cleared, Doscare's body was charred and lifeless.

Thomas's eyes rolled into the back of his head, and he fell to the ground. Hexia quickly caught him and eased his descent to the ground.

"Thomas! Thomas! Brother!" Gerum screamed in fear. "Hexia, what happened?"

"He tapped into the legendary ice dragon. It is a spell no mortal can hope to survive as it drains your life energy to power the dragon. He is dying."

Gerum began to cry. "Help him," he cried out as Hexia looked at him with tears flowing like a river.

"I'm not going to lose him." In that moment, Hexia removed a small vial from her pocket and opened it. Then with no words, she drained the contents into Thomas's blood-covered mouth.

"What is—"

"Be quiet," she cut off Gerum. "It's my soul. I'm going to use it to heal Thomas."

"But you're immortal. Losing your soul won't kill you, will it?" Gerum asked.

With tears in her eyes, she looked at Gerum. "No, but it will make me mortal."

Hexia channeled the soul all through Thomas's body, repairing everything it could. After this, Hexia looked at Gerum. "It's done. It's up to him now."

Gerum said, "Hexia, your body…you're a beautiful woman, but why are you so pale?"

Just then, Hexia collapsed, and the two were unconscious. Gerum built a fire, brought all their supplies, and made camp where they were.

C H A P T E R

11

THREE DAYS HAD passed, and Thomas awakened in a daze. "What happened?" In a blur, Thomas could make out Gerum, and in a raspy voice, he said, "Gerum."

"Don't move, Thomas. Drink this. It's water."

"What happened, Gerum?"

"You and Hexia fought Doscare, and you won."

"That's great, now we can—"

Gerum put his hands up. "Don't, Thomas. You and Hexia won, but you were dying. That last attack took all your strength, and so Hexia…" He looked over at Hexia's now floating body.

"Hexia?" Thomas leaned over.

"Don't touch her, Thomas. She's still healing."

"What did she do, Gerum?" he asked, looking worried.

"She gave you her power to beat Doscare and then gave you her soul to stay alive. You both have been asleep for three days. The day after the battle, I woke to see her floating like that. She is healing herself now that she does not have her soul," Gerum explained carefully. "Here, eat." Gerum handed Thomas a bowl of food.

"So her soul is in me now?" Thomas asked.

"Yes, in a sense. I'm sure your own soul absorbed hers, and now you're not only alive, but you might be stronger as well. As far as the ten pressure stones, I have all I need and more, and I even enchanted your armor," Gerum explained. "After you attacked Doscare, your armor itself turned sapphire blue and is embedded with his white magic. So your armor is now blue with the white dragon on it. It is the white ice dragon's armor, which is tougher and more resilient to all white magic. I would say your only weakness now is dark magic, but no one on Earth could match you in power." Gerum continued, "After we eat, I will get to forging your sword. It will take a month to forge, but it will be the best sword in the whole kingdom. As for you, rest, brother, and watch over Hexia. I'll prepare food for her once she's ready."

Two more days passed, and Thomas didn't move from Hexia's side. Suddenly, her eyes sprang open, and the floating pod burst open with green water.

"Hexia!" Thomas ran toward her, only to turn around quickly. "Oh my lord."

Hexia blinked her eyes. "What?" As she stood up, she looked down to realize she was naked, and her whole curvy, voluptuous body was on display for the world.

About this time, Gerum returned from hunting and saw Hexia. "Oh my god, you're beautiful!" Gerum shouted out.

Hexia threw up water and put on a robe of animal skin in a flash. "You perverts, both of you." In her embarrassment, she used her magic to turn the soup that was over the fire into tentacles and slapped Gerum and Thomas on the back. They both cried out in pain. She then spun and formed clothes, covering herself.

Hexia looked at Thomas. "Are you alright, Thomas?"

"Yes, thanks to you. Why did you do that, Hexia? You're a mortal now, aren't you?" he asked, feeling a twinge of guilt.

"I am, but if I didn't, you would have died. I owed you that. And, Gerum, I owe you this for taking care of us both." She walked over to Gerum's water barrel and placed her hand in it. Suddenly, the water blasted up and turned from a clear color to a radiant sapphire as Gerum and Thomas looked in amazement.

"Wow, are you sure, Hexia?" Gerum asked.

"Of course," Hexia replied.

"What is it, Gerum?" Thomas asked, confused.

"Hexia not only blessed the water but this is rare sapphire water. It's water that can only be blessed and purified by a true water goddess. This, to a smith, is rarer than all of the jewels in the kingdom. With this water, I can make you the legendary black dragon blade. It will give you a whole new set of power. Thank you so much, Hexia—I mean, sister."

Hexia blushed. "You're welcome, brother."

"Oh, I forgot I made food!" Gerum paused. "Well, I had made food until sister used it to slap us properly." Everyone laughed at this revelation.

"Come on, Hexia," Thomas said, laughing. "Let us make the food. You rest, Gerum. You took care of us. Now let us take care of you."

"Ah, a day off. Time for sunburn," Gerum stated, laughing.

"If you get sunburned, I'm not healing you!" Hexia yelled over her shoulder as she and Thomas ran off to the woods.

Gerum, lying there, suddenly remembered. *Wait a minute, we have a stockpile we don't need.* He paused and smiled, his eyes turning blood red again. He closed his eyes and fell asleep.

Thomas and Hexia were walking through the woods when Hexia stopped, realizing they had plenty of food. Just then, her thoughts were interrupted by wet lips upon hers. *He's kissing me,* Hexia thought and blushed as she closed her eyes.

"What was that for?" Hexia asked.

"A thank-you for saving my life."

Hexia, her face turning red, asked Thomas, "Do you love me?"

Thomas, releasing her face, just smiled. "We better get back. I'm sure Gerum has figured out by now we have enough food." He turned to start walking.

Hexia grabbed him and gave him one more passionate kiss, and the two ran off laughing the whole way back. Upon arriving, they made a huge pot of food, and the aroma awakened Gerum.

"What smells so delicious?" he asked, breathing in the amazing aroma.

"Mountain lion stew with all the good parts," Thomas answered, his mouth watering.

"Yum, yum," Gerum answered and made himself the biggest bowl of the three. With full bellies, no one went to sleep; instead, they stayed up talking about the next month.

"So tomorrow you will make the sword, Gerum?" Thomas asked.

"Yes, and I will need the whole month to be left alone so I can make it properly. The dragon tooth chunk may look like a lot, but if done right, it will be just enough to make the sword. What about you, Thomas?" Gerum asked.

"Well, I don't know. Let me see where I am at." Thomas decided to try on the new sapphire dragon armor and concentrated. Out of nowhere, snow began to fall and spin like a tornado in the distance. "Wow, I don't even feel the effects of the magic anymore. This is incredible."

Hexia retorted, *You're welcome, lover boy,* in Thomas's mind and looked at him in a teasing manner.

"Okay," Thomas answered. "Then it's settled. Hexia and I will train together this month while you work on the sword."

12

As the month flew by, Hexia and Thomas became closer. Due to the training, Thomas could now make smaller ice dragons and use them like missiles, as well as create white magic shields like Doscare and use white magic beams. Thomas was even able to wrap Hexia's goddess and monster forms in white magic armor. Both his and Hexia's powers had increased dramatically. Thomas could also make ice weapons, and wielding an ice long sword, he swung at Hexia with lightning speed. Hexia, using the magic armor, shattered the sword, and Thomas summoned another one in the blink of an eye.

"Let's rest and wash up. Gerum should be almost done with the sword." The two embraced in a long kiss and made for the river.

Gerum, on the other hand, was covered in soot and had lost many pounds due to the sweat and heat.

"Come on!" Gerum yelled as he pulled a giant black blade out of the furnace and into the water. The blade quickly shrank, and a huge cloud of smoke flew into the air.

"It's finished!" Gerum shouted just as Thomas and Hexia arrived. Fire bellowed like a white-hot tower, then quickly turned black. Smoke covered the whole area, and through the coughing and blurred vision, Thomas and Hexia looked up to see Gerum holding a hulking buster sword. The sleek black blade and purple handle with a black diamond gem on the hilt shone with purple radiant light.

Hexia and Thomas were dumbfounded at the massive blade.

"That's incredible!" Thomas shouted as he gazed at his new sword.

Gerum, looking like ashy death, said, "This is my finest work, brother, but it is very heavy. Here, try it out."

Thomas took the hilt in both hands and, even with super strength, barely managed to lift the giant blade. "Wow, this is huge, Gerum. You couldn't make it smaller?" Thomas groaned as he tried to hold the sword straight.

"I'm sorry, brother, but this is the legendary black dragon blade. This blade has to be big as it harnesses the darkness of a person and increases their magical resistance to dark magic. It also increases one's strength a thousandfold, hence the large size. Try embracing your darker side and see what happens."

"I don't think so," Hexia interjected. "How can you be so sure Thomas can resist the power, Gerum?"

"I don't know if he can, dear sister, but I have faith in my brother. Go ahead, Thomas," Gerum answered.

Thomas closed his eyes and let a wave of dark purple energy wash over him. Suddenly, Thomas's eyes turned a sleek dark purple color, and he sported a monstrous grin as he slashed the sword like it weighed nothing. A wave of dark energy flew like lightning and destroyed everything in its path. Thomas turned to face Hexia and Gerum, began to drool while smiling, and started to laugh.

"The power, the power, the power," Thomas chanted as he raised the sword at the two. Gerum quickly threw a pressure stone at the sword, and as it exploded right at Thomas's face, Thomas fell down, and the sword slammed into the ground.

"He went berserk, didn't he, Gerum?"

"Yes, sister, I am afraid so. He will need another month of training before we are ready to leave."

The next morning, Thomas awoke with the sword away from him. "What happened?" he asked.

"You have got to stop making this a habit," said Hexia, smiling.

"I fainted again, didn't I?" Thomas sighed. "I swear it seems like any new power I get almost kills me," he said in anger.

"Well, you're human, after all. You're a mortal dealing with supernatural powers. Of course, it is not going to be easy, Thomas." Hexia tried to comfort him, and it worked.

"Okay, where's the black dragon sword?"

"It's over there. Gerum has it," Hexia replied.

Thomas reached for the sword only to have his hand grabbed by Gerum.

"Brother, are you sure you're okay?"

"I'm fine," he answered and grabbed the sword by the hilt. This time, however, he was instantly overtaken by the power and began to see purple. He quickly let go of the hilt, startled and surprised.

"How can I wield this sword, Gerum?" he asked.

"According to legend, the user of the black dragon blade must be one with his dark side."

Upon this realization, Thomas closed his eyes and embraced his dark side. Suddenly, dark purple energy began to radiate around Thomas, and he opened his eyes and grabbed the hilt of the sword. With one hand, Thomas lifted the heavy blade and swung it in the air, releasing a black dragon of power. The dragon flew into the air like a cannon and exploded with a wave of power that had never been seen before. Looking at Thomas, both Gerum and Hexia noticed that this time he was calm, but the aura was murderous.

Thomas looked back at the duo with a murderous smile and said, "Let's kill the dragon." At this point, Thomas's eyes rolled into the back of his skull, and he collapsed. Hexia held Thomas, and Gerum grabbed the sword. She noticed it was not affecting Gerum the same as it affected Thomas.

"Tell me something, Gerum, why does the sword not affect you like it does Thomas?" she asked.

He looked at her with an evil grin and began to laugh maniacally. "You think it doesn't? I built it, so I am familiar with every facet of this blade. I only manage it better." As he spoke, Gerum wrapped the hilt in a cloth and placed it against a tree.

Hexia checked and noticed Thomas's energy was low, but he was okay. A few hours later, Thomas awakened to the smell of a delicious stew.

"My, that smells delicious," he said with drool coming out of his mouth.

Without another word, Hexia handed him a big bowl. "Eat, Thomas."

Without words, he downed the bowl in seconds.

"That's amazing, but what happened?" Thomas looked at Gerum, who sat there and said nothing, and then at Hexia, who looked concerned and decided to answer.

"You failed to wield the sword again, Thomas, and this time you fainted," she explained. "The power needed to harness the sword comes from your dark energy and your life force. Using it too much or releasing too much energy can kill you, Thomas," Gerum explained in a worried tone.

"Let's eat and rest for tonight, and tomorrow I can begin to train you," Gerum said.

With no more words from anyone, the three ate their fill, and Thomas and Gerum fell asleep.

Hexia, in her curiosity, approached the black blade. "I have to know what Gerum used to make this sword so powerful." Hexia grabbed the sword, and using her power, she began to inspect the blade. As if the blade sensed the intrusion from Hexia, it began to glow dark purple, and she felt the presence of a dark demonic force within the sword. Suddenly, she was thrown with unbelievable force away from the sword and almost lost her footing. Hexia's left arm was burnt, which she quickly healed as she said, "So there is a demon in the sword. That's where the power comes from. It drains Thomas's life force and releases power. I have to destroy this demon, even if it costs me my life." Hexia ran back, turned into a water spirit, and entered the sword.

"Who enters my home?" a large, loud, and evil voice came from the darkness.

"I am Hexia, goddess of water and lover to your master."

"Impossible, little spirit. My master has no lover. I am Gravex, and this blade was forged by my master. I was sent here to offer my infinite power to the user. I believe I am doing just that," Gravex explained.

"Who is your master, and is the one called Thomas the user you speak of?"

"I do not know any names, but the great black dragon god made me, and he told me to serve the user of the sword."

"That's not possible." Hexia quickly explained to Gravex, "A smith named Gerum made your home. Sure, he has some dark tendencies, but he is far from the black dragon god of legend. The black dragon god Zerok was a master of magic and was able to command armies of demons like yourself. He could also turn the minds of any heroes to dust with a thought and was defeated thousands of years ago by the golden dragon, Narvaria, and her noble knights of light. Gerum seems malicious, but he's nothing like that."

Gravex just listened and laughed. "You are young, water goddess. I know who you are, and trust me, this will not end the way you think it will. The user may use my power, and I will not drain him any further. Tomorrow, with the rise of the sun, he will be able to wield the blade and me with ease and clarity, but in exchange, I have a proposition for you."

Hexia looked into the darkness in concern and shouted, "I don't make deals with those I cannot see, Gravex, and yes, I can read your mind, demon." Just then, the abyss began to shake, and a giant four-armed demon with horns like a devil appeared towering over the small Hexia.

"Here is my offer. The user may use my power unhindered, and in exchange, you will become my pet and serve me here in the abyss of the sword."

"No way!" she shouted. "I will never be your pet, but I will offer you this: let Thomas use you as he wishes, and in return, I will make a clone of myself, and the clone will serve you in my place."

Gravex thought for a minute and replied, "Very well, let's begin."

Hexia grew to her full adult form and began to construct her clone as Gravex looked on with anticipation. He began to growl with excitement. When the clone was complete, it approached the demon and knelt, addressing Gravex as master. This pleased the demon greatly, but Hexia still did not trust him. Without a second's notice, she asked, "So is our deal good, and if so, prove it."

"Fine." The demon stood up and began to chant a spell. A moment later, a symbol was burned into Hexia's right hand.

"Eh, what is this?" she asked as she winced in pain.

"That is my demonic symbol," Gravex explained. "In the event I do not keep to the bargain, you may summon me out of the blade for everyone, including the user, to see. I will submit to your orders and only yours."

Hexia was surprised. *This is the first demon with honor I have ever met. Maybe we can use him to fight the sword master,* she thought.

"Alright, Gravex, you have what you want, so I will be off." With no more words, Hexia pulled her water spirit back to notice her hand bore the demonic symbol. She then sat by the sword and began to circulate energy. As she did, she could not help but think, *What if Zerok is alive? No, that's impossible. He was destroyed, wasn't he?*

The next morning, Thomas and Gerum awoke at the same time, and this time, Thomas made breakfast for everyone.

"Good morning, Hexia," Thomas said as he looked over at the goddess.

"Um, good morning, Thomas. How did you sleep?"

"I slept great," Thomas replied. "How did you fare last night?"

Hexia held her hand with the demon mark. "It was fine. Quiet as usual."

"Good. Today we can train with the sword again, Thomas," Gerum quickly reminded him. "The sword master will be only a few miles up, so we must get you ready and in fighting shape."

With no words, Thomas got up and walked over to the sword. Grabbing it by the hilt, he threw it up in the air. He jumped and caught it, only to find there were no draining effects. On the contrary, he felt purple energy flowing into him.

"This is amazing!" Thomas exclaimed in excitement. He swung the sword, which now felt lighter than air to him. With a thought, Thomas swung the sword and released a dark purple wave that cut down half of the trees in front of him. In his excitement, he spun the sword and put it on his back.

"This is great! It's lighter than my old sword."

13

As the team set out, Thomas waved his new sword in front of himself, amazed at every facet of the blade. "This is incredible. I don't know what's different, but I have complete control over the sword. It's almost as if the blade has a power in it, and overnight it just decided to listen to me," Thomas explained with revelation.

Hexia just rolled her eyes, thinking to herself, *If he only knew the lengths that I went to for that sword, he would marry me on the spot.* Suddenly, Thomas stopped and looked at her.

"What lengths and marry you?" Thomas asked, puzzled at Hexia's thoughts.

Hexia sighed. "Oh crap, I forgot about the mind link we share. Okay, Thomas, let me explain. I looked deep into that sword while you were asleep and discovered it houses a demon put there by the black dragon god."

At this, both Thomas and Gerum stopped dead in their tracks and looked back at Hexia in confusion and curiosity.

"There's really a demon in there?" asked Gerum, astonished at this news.

"And what did you do to quell this demon, Hexia?" Thomas finished the curious questioning.

"I offered it a clone of myself who serves him, and in exchange, he follows you and you can use his power without restraint," she explained. "Also"—she looked at Gerum suspiciously—"since we're on the subject, Gerum, how did you trap a demon in that sword? And don't lie to me."

"Honestly, I don't know. Forging the sword can allow for demons to appear as it is a dark blade, but as far as one being in the sword, I have no idea," Gerum responded.

"It told me it was put there by the black dragon god," Hexia said while raising a water axe.

"I swear I don't know anything about that. The black dragon, Zerok, has been destroyed for centuries. How could it have been put there by that monster?" Gerum explained in shock.

Just as Hexia was about to swing at Gerum, Thomas quickly intervened. "Hexia, stop this now!" Thomas screamed as he put the sword between Hexia and Gerum. "This is no time for us to be fighting each other. I have known Gerum all my life. He is a brother to me. Also, I'm in your debt for the sword. We let you live, and you allowed me to use the sword like a master, so we're even now. Let it go."

The group stood in silence for a minute, then continued walking, an uncomfortable aura surrounding them.

After a few hours of silence, they came to a rocky area and heard the sound of snoring. "Zzzzzzzzzzz, ccchhhhhhhooooooo, zzzzzzzzzzzzz ccchhooooooo."

"Who's sleeping?" Thomas asked rhetorically. As if hearing him, an old man woke up with a cough and came out from behind a rock.

"I was, youngster. Who are you, and what do you want?"

"Old man, we're looking for a master swordsman who guards the golden dragon. Can you tell us if you know who he is?"

Looking at the three travelers, the old man's gaze turned to Hexia. "My, my, a water goddess, and a true beauty at that. May I ask your name, my dear?" the old man asked, completely ignoring Thomas and Gerum.

"Uh, it's Hexia. And you are?"

"I am Trebonas, master swordsman of the realm and eternal guardian of the golden dragon."

In shock, Thomas quickly pulled out his sword. "What! You're the master swordsman? I have come to defeat you, Trebonas."

"Shut up!" The swordsman looked over, and with a *whoosh*, the wind seemed to gust at Thomas and Gerum. A moment later, Gerum went to raise his arm and realized it was gone.

"Aaaaaahhhhhh!" he shouted. Thomas quickly spun around and saw Gerum's lifeless arm on the ground, blood beginning to flow. He quickly stopped the bleeding using his belt. By the time he looked back, Trebonas was at Hexia's side, looking her up and down in an inappropriate manner, as if he was undressing her with his eyes.

"Oh my goddess, it has been so long since I have seen a woman. What do you say you come with me, stay here, and in turn, I'll let your friends live?"

Disgusted by the old man, Hexia drew back her hand and slapped him hard across his face.

"I guess that's a no," Trebonas replied with a smile.

Without warning, he opened his sword and sheathed it again. As it closed, a hundred slashes appeared on Hexia, slicing her body to pieces.

"Oh well, you win some, you lose some," Trebonas said, looking at Hexia as she began to rebuild herself. Trebonas looked at Thomas and asked, "What, boy, you want some too? Just try and fight me. No mortal has ever survived me in a fight."

As he was speaking, Trebonas opened his sword, but this time it was met with an invisible force of resistance.

"Oh, what's this?" Trebonas looked at Thomas. "Oh, I see, telekinesis. Well, try this." Trebonas leaped into the air, waved his cloak, and disappeared.

By this time, Hexia had rebuilt herself and created a water clone to aid Thomas. Thomas, in a rage, swung his sword, destroying the landscape. *Where is he?* he thought. Suddenly, out of nowhere, a blade came inches from his face. He quickly blocked with the dragon blade and dodged to the side; however, Thomas got a deep wound on his right shoulder.

"You're going to have to do better than that!" Trebonas said, masked by the dust and debris from Thomas's attack.

"Then try this, old man!" Thomas used telekinesis to turn small stones into hundreds of projectiles. He quickly jumped and fired them all at once at the ground around him. Trebonas also leaped into the air as Thomas exclaimed with a "Got ya!" He slashed his massive blade, and a purple wave fired at Trebonas with incredible force. Trebonas slashed back at the wave and in an instant, cut the wave in half.

"Not bad, kid, but you've got another thousand years to be my equal." Trebonas turned himself into two clones, and all three slashed with the same force back at Thomas. Thomas used water armor and blocked the attack but was blown to the ground with insane speed. Thomas slammed into the ground with a boom, and as he stood up, he was covered in thousands of tiny cuts all over his body. He coughed up blood. "Damn, if I had not blocked that, I would be dead for sure."

Just then, Hexia came running to Thomas. "Are you alright?" she asked in concern, seeing the cuts all over his body.

"I'm okay. Can you heal me?" he asked.

"Of course," she replied as she put him into a water ball that immediately started to heal him. Then she turned into her first form and attacked Trebonas with a bullet barrage of water spikes. Trebonas, blocking them, mocked Hexia.

"See, girl, if you chose me, you wouldn't have to be fighting now. I could protect you from all." With a smile, Trebonas sent another wave of air at Hexia that cut through all her attacks and sliced her into pieces again. Luckily, this was her clone; however, it fell out of the sky with a loud thunderous bang.

Hexia, breathing hard now from fighting, turned into her monster form and prepared to fight Trebonas again.

"You think that monster form is going to stop me, little girl?" Trebonas mocked her as he covered himself and disappeared again. However, Hexia, in this form, could easily follow him. Using her tentacles, she ensnared him and began to squeeze the life out of him.

"What? How did you catch me?" Trebonas asked while trying to breathe and move out of Hexia's grasp.

"I am a goddess, and I could easily follow you in this form. You're no match for me," Hexia replied.

"Oh, you think so, little goddess? Try this." Trebonas went limp in the tentacles, and with yellow in his eyes, he shouted, "Makrebonestrobus." In an instant, Hexia exploded and fell into her human form.

Oh no, he knows magic, Hexia thought in concern.

Trebonas, with his eyes still yellow, looked at Hexia and commanded, "Reductousinfame." Upon this magical command, his sword turned into one thousand swords and flew at Hexia and the team with extreme speed.

Out of nowhere, a wave of blue and purple came flying and destroyed the swords.

"What's this?" Trebonas looked in astonishment. As the smoke cleared, Thomas came into view with a horn on his head and his eyes purple.

"This mortal's body is amazing, Hexia. Why didn't you tell me I had such a wonderful new master?"

Hexia, looking in confusion, suddenly realized the person in front of her was none other than Gravex in Thomas's body. In horror, she screamed, "Gravex, what are you doing? You promised to follow Thomas, not possess him!"

Gravex looked at Hexia and replied, "I'm saving his life while you heal his injuries. I can use his body to fight the old man. Besides, we have a history."

"Excuse me?" Hexia asked in surprise. "What do you mean, history?"

"This is Trebonas, the man who defeated me and claimed my sword power for himself a thousand years ago. I owe him a rematch." Just then, Gravex, in Thomas's body, swung the blade in a circular motion, and a giant black dragon flew toward Trebonas.

"What the hell!" Trebonas was instantly blown back and slammed into the rocks below with the force of a bomb. Trebonas, quickly standing up, looked at Thomas and said, "Hey, who are you, lad? That attack was Gravex's attack. How do you know it?"

Gravex, looking at the old man and with blood falling out of the corner of his mouth, smiled and said, "Because I am Gravex, you old fool, and you will give me back all my power."

Gravex flew at Trebonas, and they clashed with their swords. The attacks were so powerful that the rocky area was instantly turned into a field of rubble. The two matched each other blow for blow for what seemed like hours until one attack from Gravex sent Trebonas flying into the rubble.

"You see, old man, you may be immortal, but I know your weakness. If I take your head, you will die, and I will claim all the power you stole." Gravex laughed manically. He suddenly stopped gloating and vomited a mouthful of blood. "Damn, this body won't hold much longer."

At this revelation, Gravex looked over at Hexia, who has collapsed from trying to heal Thomas throughout the whole fight. "This ends now, old man!" Gravex shouted as he flew into the air and created an earth-size energy ball, preparing for a final attack.

At this moment, Trebonas flew into the air, and with a glowing yellow light around him, he began to chant a spell. As the orb of power condensed into a small ball on the tip of the black dragon blade, a small, condensed orb appeared on Trebonas's sword. The power from both attacks turned the ground to dust and sand even before they moved.

"It's over!" Gravex yelled as he flew toward the old man with unreal speed. At the same time, Trebonas, with no words, swung his sword with all his might. The two powers collided and began to disintegrate the mountain area. Gerum hurriedly grabbed Hexia and tried to flee the area, barely making it in time before a massive crater emerged where they had just been.

In the middle of the crater were both Gravex and Trebonas, not moving and not facing each other. Just then, Thomas's arms and legs fell off his body, and his torso hit the ground with a thud. At the same time, Trebonas just smiled and said, "Well, Gravex, I'd say you won this round. Maybe in hell we can fight again."

In the next moment, Trebonas dropped his sword and caught his own head as it fell into his hands, and his body went limp.

Gravex used the last of his power to put Thomas back together and healed him before returning to the sword. Thomas and Hexia came to with no memory of the fight.

What happened? they both thought as they sat in the now quiet area of debris.

Thomas, linking to Hexia, thought, *I remember fighting, then everything going black.*

Hexia replied, *I remember the demon taking over your body and fighting the old man.*

As they sat in silence, a yellowish-purple light began to shine from Trebonas's body. This light quickly flew and entered the black dragon blade. In another instant, the blade transformed into a normal long sword with the hilt a solid gold and the blade outlining a dragon in gold etched into it.

Gerum, who was eating a healing root, looked at the sword in amazement and shouted, "The black dragon blade's true form! You did it, Thomas!"

With no words, Thomas focused on the sword and said, "Demon, come out. I wish to speak with you." Gravex slid out of the sword in a weak and weary manner. "Yes, my lord."

"You saved my life and defeated this enemy. To me, you are free. All I ask is you leave a sliver of your power in the sword that I may use to slay the golden dragon."

"I cannot accept," Gravex replied. "However, I will replicate the sword for myself and follow you. I swore an oath, and even though I am a demon, I still have honor."

"Agreed. You may return to the sword to recover, but once your strength is restored, you may return and walk with us if you like."

"Thank you, master. Please accept this as a token of my gratitude." Gravex grabbed Thomas's hand and began to chant. Suddenly, an extreme burning pain was felt in Thomas's left hand and arm.

"What is this?" Thomas asked, wincing in pain. A moment later, Gravex stopped chanting.

"This is a soul seal. I have bound myself to you. You can summon me with a thought, and I can take over your body if you're in need of my power again."

After the burning dissipated, Thomas nodded in understanding. "Then you may return to the sword and rest, and I will summon you when I need you."

Without another word, Gravex jumped back into the sword, and the sword returned to its glowing magnificence.

Coming out of the crater, Thomas looked upon his fallen comrades. "Oh no, Hexia, Gerum!" he shouted, running to their aid.

Hexia, looking translucent, said, "Thomas, I am fading. I need to rest," before collapsing. As soon as Hexia hit the ground, a water fountain lifted her body and put her into the green cocoon as before. Thomas looked at Gerum, who was pale from blood loss. "Are you okay, brother?"

Gerum just looked at Thomas with a sarcastic smile. "Oh yeah, I'm dandy," he said, laughing and coughing the entire time.

"Let me make a fire, and we can cauterize the wound, Gerum." Without any more words, Thomas made a fire and burned Gerum's nub. Screaming in pain, Gerum fell and passed out due to shock. Thomas did not say anything but only made enough food for a small family. When Gerum awoke, night had already fallen, and Thomas had fallen asleep from exhaustion and a full belly. Gerum smelled the food, ate like he hadn't eaten in days, then passed back out.

Five days passed, and the two only woke to eat and use the bathroom, then went back to sleep. On the sixth day, Hexia woke up Thomas and Gerum. "Hey, wake up, you two."

"Hexia, you're awake! Are you okay?" Gerum asked.

"Yes, I am all better. But how are you, Gerum?"

"Well, I am lighter," he replied, laughing, "but I am okay. I'm lucky I only lost my arm and not something more important."

Hexia made a vomiting sound and turned to Thomas. "What about you, Thomas? Are you okay?"

"I'm okay. We have been resting. I'm glad you're okay now. I was worried."

"Well, what's on the agenda for today?" Hexia asked.

"We begin to march for the peak and for the golden dragon. There is nothing in our way now, at least I hope not," Thomas replied in excitement.

Once everyone packed up and began to walk, the team traveled many miles before reaching a cold point on the mountain.

"It's freezing up here. I'm going to turn to ice," Hexia complained, shivering.

Without a word, Thomas used his energy to create a barrier around Hexia, blocking the cold. "Is that better, Hexia?"

"Yes, thank you, Thomas," Hexia replied.

In the fogged area, the team noticed a bright golden castle just a stone's throw away.

"We're almost there," Thomas said with anticipation.

As the trio reached the door of the snow-covered castle, each one readied for the fight: Thomas grabbed the black dragon blade, Gerum grabbed his crossbow, and Hexia created two water balls in her hands. With a powerful kick, Thomas blasted open the door to the castle, and they ran in screaming, "Aaaaaahhhhhhhhh!" As they reached the center of the castle, all was quiet.

Where is everyone? Thomas linked to Hexia.

I don't know.

About that time, Gerum yelled in the distance, "I found something!" Thomas followed the sound of Gerum's voice, and they reached the throne room where a small note rested on the throne. Thomas opened the note to read it.

> You have come far and wide, travelers. However, I am not here. I am being held captive by the first king. Yes, the first king is alive and has taken me as his queen to ensure no one can see me and use me to usurp his power. I know this has been a long journey for you, yet I must ask you to please come to the castle, defeat the king, and free me. If you do, I will grant you any wish you desire. I know this is a lot to ask, but I will be forever in your debt.
>
> Signed, the Golden Dragon, Narvaria

CHAPTER

14

In a rage, Thomas screamed out and threw the letter to the ground. "The waste of time with this journey only to find out she is my queen. I will kill her for this."

Out of nowhere, Gerum began to laugh hysterically. "So that's where you are, dear sister. After all these years, I will come to the castle, and I will kill you and claim the world for myself."

Thomas and Hexia looked at Gerum in surprise. "Brother, what are you talking about?"

"Shut up, fool! I am not your brother. I merely followed you to find my dear sister."

At this point, Gerum began to glow purple, and with a grunting and squeezing noise, he began to transform. The arm that was cut off was replaced by a giant black and silver claw, and Gerum arose to become fifty feet tall. A tail with spikes came flying out and knocked Hexia against the wall with a bang. Wings sprouted with spikes on the edges, and Gerum's whole body became covered with black scales. His face exploded to reveal a monstrous dragon face with three rows of razor-sharp teeth, a nose that breathed fire, and horns to rival a true dragon god.

Thomas, in shock, asked, "Who are you, dragon? Answer me."

"Foolish mortal! I am Zerok, the true dragon god and soon ruler of this world. Thanks to you, I will kill Narvaria and plunge the world into darkness."

Zerok spread his massive wings, blasted into the air with lightning speed, and took off, leaving Thomas and Hexia in the rubble. Thomas resurfaced and screamed out in pain and anger. *I am truly a fool. All this time I never knew. There is no point in fighting. There is no point in going on. I cannot beat a dragon god.*

Hexia, resurfacing from the debris, could hear Thomas's thoughts and his despair, and she was left speechless. With no words, Hexia came to Thomas's side and held him as he cried deeply in her arms. Thomas was truly defeated.

Thomas spent hours in Hexia's arms. As Hexia tried to comfort him, his sadness and sorrow turned to anger and rage. Hexia looked to Thomas. "Now that the truth has been revealed, Thomas, what are we going to do?"

With tears still in his eyes, he looked at Hexia. "I'm going to kill Zerok and the king and Narvaria. Come on, Hexia, we're going to the castle."

Thomas picked up his sword and summoned Gravex.

"Yes, master," Gravex replied in horror as he saw the anger boiling in Thomas's eyes.

"Can you use your power to teleport us to the king's castle?" Thomas asked in anger.

"Sadly, no, master, but I can teleport you just outside the castle. The king's castle seems to be protected by some magical barrier."

"That will be fine, Gravex. Send us there and leave the barrier to me."

With a wave of his hand, Gravex sent Hexia and Thomas outside the gate to the king's castle. Hexia hid behind Thomas and said quietly, "I sense a dark evil here, Thomas. Be careful."

Thomas, with no words, held up the black dragon blade and began to glow a red aura that Hexia had never seen before. This was pure anger and malice, and it scared her to her core. Thomas swung the sword down, and a huge black wave slammed into an invisible barrier, and lightning shot everywhere like a waterfall of power. Without warning, an explosion of power blasted away something, and Hexia smiled with her eyes turning red. "We're going to kill them all."

As Thomas's anger flowed through him, it began to cover Hexia in a red aura just like Thomas, and with red eyes, they both stepped into the castle gates and headed for the castle door. Without words, the two battled every knight that came their way and killed everyone. Blood began to flow like a river as they slashed, drowned, and impaled everyone. No man, woman, or child was safe from their wrath.

As they approached the door to the castle, Thomas and Hexia's forms began to resemble demons with horns, claws, and scales beginning to form on Thomas's body. Hexia was adorned with a crown of blood ice, with her once golden hair now red and thorny, her white robe replaced by a red dress of blood ice, and her teeth becoming razor-sharp. With wings of ice, they destroyed the door with unbelievable force.

Making their way up the castle stairs, they were met with no resistance until they reached the throne room. It was a wide, large room able to fit ten houses inside. They saw two thrones at the end of the room, with giant black curtains making the room look like the dark abyss. In one throne, there was a rotting skeleton, and the other was empty. Thomas and Hexia blasted huge waves of blood ice and dark power at the throne, blasting them into pieces. With drool flowing down the mouths of the demonic couple, the room went silent.

"Enough, you impudent worms!" a loud voice rang out, shaking the whole foundation of the castle. This voice sent fire into Thomas and Hexia as they began to blast waves of destruction around the entire room.

"Hahahaha, you fools can't harm me." Out of nowhere, a huge skeletal hand grabbed Thomas and slammed him into the wall while Hexia watched in horror as Thomas's body went limp and reverted back to his human form.

Hexia, now angrier than ever, turned into a demonic giant form never seen before. She sent a blast of blood ice at the abyss and revealed the skeletal hand's owner. This gigantic black skeleton wore only a king's crown on his head and had eyes like blue sapphires. He lunged for Hexia, grabbed her demon goddess form, and slammed her just as he did Thomas. She screamed out in pain as there appeared to be a magical barrier around the king. Once Hexia was reduced back to normal, the giant skeleton turned to human form and spoke.

"I am king of this land. You weaklings will never defeat me. Why are you here?"

Thomas, now awake and moving, looked in horror at the black figure and coughed up a mouthful of blood.

"Your Majesty, we have come to kill the golden dragon queen, Narvaria."

"And why is this?" asked the king.

"We believe the black dragon god is going to kill her, steal her power, and rule this land, and that includes you, my lord," Thomas explained.

"That is impossible," the king replied. "I have the black dragon's soul. Narvaria and I defeated him and destroyed him. He's gone."

"Oh, is that so," a disembodied voice rang out in the dark room as Zerok appeared in Gerum's form.

"Who the hell are you?" the king bellowed as he looked in anger at the uninvited guest.

Thomas and Hexia looked in anger as well.

"It's you, Gerum, or should we call you Zerok, you monster!" she yelled out.

Zerok laughed at the duo.

"Well, well, if it isn't my old friends. Welcome. Looks like we're all here, so, Thomas, I will be taking all your power now, okay."

"And how are you going to do that, Zerok?" he yelled out while shooting a wave of purple power at Zerok.

As Zerok easily destroyed the wave, he laughed and explained to Thomas, "I made your armor not to give *you* power, but *me*. Like this. *Expandeiance!*" The magic spell rang out, and Thomas's armor fell off him, flew, and formed perfectly to Zerok's body.

"Now for that sword. Redemtious." The black dragon blade turned white hot, forcing Thomas to drop it, and it flew over to Zerok.

"Ah, that's better," Zerok said happily.

"Who are you?" asked the king.

"Oh, you don't recognize me? How about this?" Zerok quickly transformed into his dragon form and easily took up all the space in the room.

Thomas was drained, Hexia frozen in fear, and the king dumb-founded at the revelation.

"I am alive!" He laughed. "And now all I need is my soul, Your Majesty." Zerok lunged and ate the skeletal king and without warning, spat out a now white-as-snow skeleton.

With Zerok now at full power, he transformed into a smaller dragon-Gerum hybrid and spoke to Thomas and Hexia.

"You were both my friends, so I will let you go. Narvaria is not here, but I will find her, and when I kill her, I will take her power and rule this land forever. Now I am going to her castle, and if you wish to try and fight me, you may find me. However, I have one surprise if you do, Thomas."

Zerok turned back into his black dragon form and flew out of the castle, destroying the room and covering Hexia and Thomas in the debris.

Thomas, now powerless, got up and pulled Hexia from the rubble.

"Come on, Hexia. Let us go. My quest is finally over."

"Excuse me, this is not the Thomas I know and came to love. He does not give up."

"But I am powerless, Hexia. I can't fight Zerok or anyone. What am I to do?"

"You're going to get up, and we are going to find a way to kill Zerok."

"There is such a way," a disembodied voice rang out.

"Your Majesty!" The duo ran over to the skeletal corpse. "You're alive."

"Not for long. Zerok took his soul back. Without it, I will turn to dust. Listen, Thomas, Narvaria is dead. She died protecting me from the darkness of Zerok's soul, but it sadly was not enough. However, I still have her power stored in the void. I will use the last of my power to retrieve it. You must stop Zerok, and afterward, you must take my place as king and rule this land."

"But, Your Majesty, I never wanted to be king. This is too much, even for me," Thomas explained in shock and surprise.

"You can, and you shall now. Oblivioxious." With a wave of his hand, a dark void appeared in front of them. Out of the dark, a huge white and gold orb appeared, and the king covered Thomas in the sphere.

Thomas's body was purified, and all the evil was forced out of his body. He was also instantly healed, as was Hexia. Both felt refreshed as the sphere gave Thomas new white and gold armor, a shield with a golden dragon on the front, and a golden sword radiating with unbelievable power with four angel wings. Thomas looked like an angelic war god, and his eyes had turned white. Hexia was also turned into a more beautiful goddess with an elegant white dress. She was adorned with diamonds all over, and her hair was a beautiful blonde. Her eyes had also turned one blue and one white. A beautiful light also glowed between the pair as they flew to the mountain to destroy the black dragon once and for all.

C H A P T E R

15

As THE DUO were flying to Zerok's new castle, a huge dark figure flew at a speed faster than Thomas and Hexia, over the two, and toward the castle as well. Not sensing any evil from the creature, Thomas and Hexia did not give it a second thought and continued to fly to the mountain.

Arriving at the foot of the mountain, they sensed a dark barrier surrounding it, similar to the one around the castle. Before, Thomas had a hard time breaking this type of barrier, but this time, with the power granted by Narvaria, Thomas waved his hand, and the barrier shattered in an instant. As the two moved to the mountain, they were quickly stopped by an invisible force. This forced the two back to the ground, and it seemed like a crushing dark power began to engulf Thomas and Hexia. But just as quickly as the force came, it dissipated, and in the dark, Thomas and Hexia could hear the moaning and groaning of what sounded like a dying troll.

As Brutilis came out of the trees, he was shaking violently as it seemed his body was being held together by dark magic.

"Brutilis, what has happened to you?" Thomas yelled in surprise.

"Mighty Thomas, Zerok has resurrected all of your foes on your journey, but we are cursed corpses. We wish to die, but we can't fight it."

At this time, Brutilis sent a shock wave of telekinesis at Hexia and blasted her ten feet back as a second wave slammed into Thomas, making him fly back ten feet, landing beside Hexia.

"Please, Thomas, I can't stop myself. I'm in so much pain. Finish me," Brutilis cried out.

Thomas, regaining his balance, answered Brutilis's call. "Brutilis, you are a fine warrior, and I release your soul from this pain and torment. Embrace the light."

Swinging Thomas's mighty golden dragon sword, he sent a light that engulfed Brutilis. Brutilis smiled in happiness.

"Thank you, noble Thomas," he said as his body turned to ash and silence fell over the battlefield.

"Rest well, Brutilis. Be finally at peace," Thomas said as a tear fell down his face. In anger, he looked at Hexia. "Our foes are alive once again by Zerok's evil dark magic. We must stop this."

Hexia nodded in silence as the two flew up to the foot of the mountain. As they approached, a loud roar came booming from a dark giant figure.

"It's Tremous," Thomas explained. "Hexia, be on guard. Tremous is strong."

As he spoke, a giant boulder came flying at the two, separating them for a moment. Out of nowhere, a giant rotting fist flew at Hexia, knocking her to the ground. Hexia used her light water power to shoot a beam at the arm, instantly cutting it off.

"Kill me!" a loud roar bellowed out, and Thomas could see Tremous was more bone than flesh and being held together by dark power. Thomas, in anger, attacked Tremous with a swing of his sword, only to be knocked back by Tremous's incredible size and force.

"Please, Thomas, I can't stop. End my life, brother."

"All right, brother. I will set you free." Thomas flew up and made a halo circle around the beast and shouted, "Golden light, free my brother."

Upon command, a shower of golden light covered Tremous, and his body began to disintegrate.

"Thank you, brother," Tremous replied with a smile and held a giant thumbs-up to Thomas before turning to ashes and fading away. Thomas fell, and Hexia ran to comfort him as he screamed and cried out.

"They were all good. Everyone we faced was good at heart, and that monster corrupted their souls. I swear I'm going to make him pay." He sucked in a shuddering breath, calming himself. "Hexia, the next one is Doscare, and it took both of us to defeat him before. This time it will be harder. We must come up with a plan."

"You're right," she said, wiping the tears from Thomas's eyes.

He thought, *Let's combine our powers from the start and finish him quickly.*

As they talked, they both flew up to face Doscare. Upon reaching the pressure stones, the duo were met with a barrage of magical power.

Thomas yelled out, "Doscare, we're here to free you. Please don't make us fight you."

The beaten corpse of Doscare appeared in front of the two and said, "I'm sorry, my friend, but I have no control over my body or my power. However, I can offer to end this quickly. Let's attack with everything we have. Please, brother, offer me this noble death so I too may rest in peace."

Thomas and Hexia listened while dodging magical attacks and mind-linked, agreeing to help Doscare. Thomas yelled out to him, "Brother, we agree. Let's end this for good."

The two flew into the air, held their hands, and began to chant. A halo of light appeared around Thomas and Hexia, and they began to absorb the light, building up one major final attack. Doscare smiled an evil grin, and with tears in his eyes, he flew up and began to absorb all the darkness around him. Thomas and Hexia's bodies turned gold as Doscare's body expanded and turned purple. Suddenly, Doscare sent a massive black dragon of pure evil at Thomas and Hexia, and they retaliated with a golden dragon just as big. The two powers clashed with enough force to destroy and disintegrate the land around them.

The powers grew from both sides as Doscare's body began to burn away. He smiled and said in his mind, "Aaaahhhhhh, thank you, brother. My soul will never forget this act, and I will watch over you both." With the last of his strength, he lowered his arms and was blasted by the light, instantly disintegrating the last of the noble warrior. Thomas had no tears this time in his white eyes.

This time, he looked at Hexia. "The old man is next and then Zerok. Let's go, Hexia." Silently, she obeyed, and they flew ahead.

After some time, they reached the old man's corpse. He did not attack but turned to face the two and welcomed them.

"Welcome, you two. I know why you're here, and believe me, I am grateful. However, I can stave off this evil on my own. You two may go."

Hexia replied, "Sword master, you can't resist forever. Please allow us to help you."

After some thought, the sword master looked at Hexia and said, "My dear, if that is the case, then it should be you to finish me. You have no weapon. I will give you my sword, and my soul will be with you against the ultimate evil that has revived me. On one condition, that is."

"And what is that, sword master?" she replied.

"You must cut off my head with my sword and free my soul."

"I can't, master. You are good. I cannot slay you."

"Then consider this fight your last." The old man raised his sword and attacked Hexia while yelling at Thomas to stay back. "This is her fight."

Hexia sent waves of light only to have them sliced in half by the sword master, who disappeared at the same time. Out of nowhere, a sword strike hit Hexia and shook her light barrier. She quickly cried out and turned into her light goddess form, sending waves of light tentacles at the sword master. Invisible blades cut through the light like butter, and Hexia used the rest to ensnare the old swordsman and take his sword. The old man smiled and thought to himself, *Good child, you will make a fine warrior.*

In her sadness and anger, she grabbed the sword, and with light, she cut his head off with a clean whoosh. With his last breath, he said to Hexia, "Good girl, you will be fine." And with that, the old swordsman turned to ash as Hexia dropped the sword and fell to her knees in tears. Thomas quickly ran to comfort her, only to have her push him away with, "No, I must embrace this pain as you have."

Wiping tears from her eyes, she looked at Thomas and said, "Come, let's kill this monster once and for all."

As they reached the dark castle of Zerok, both Thomas and Hexia circulated all their power and destroyed the door. Standing in the throne room of the castle, they found Zerok awaiting them. He laughed.

"Well, look at this. My sister has been dead all along. I smell her power on you. After I take her power from you, I will rule this land."

Without words, Thomas and Hexia sent a blast of light energy, and as it hit Zerok, he cried out in pain.

"Aaaahhh! You fools will die for this. Come, Zemarkus!" Suddenly, dark clouds descended to reveal the monster amalgamation that Thomas and Gerum had seen in the village. Thomas looked in horror as Zemarkus now had one hundred heads, four legs of a dog, two tails—one of a snake and one of a scorpion—and a turtle shell on its back. The monster roared with the cries of the one hundred villagers who had been fused with animals to make its monstrous body.

Thomas quickly got ready for battle, but Hexia put her hand in front of him and said, "No, Thomas. You fight Zerok. I'll kill this monster."

As the two flew away, Zemarkus followed Hexia while Zerok destroyed the castle to fly after Thomas. "I'm going to kill you," Zerok shouted out.

"Let's see you try," Thomas shot bullets of light at Zerok as Zerok created a dark barrier.

The two slammed into each other, and with every sword swing Thomas launched, Zerok countered with his claws. Hexia, meanwhile, had turned into her first form, and her tentacles were being cut down by Zemarkus's six mutated arms. The fight raged for hours, neither side giving an inch, their powers turning the land around them to ash.

As Thomas swung his sword, it hit Zerok's shoulder, and Thomas quickly noticed a shocking revelation. *I can't and will not win.* Zerok knocked Thomas to the ground. As Thomas looked on at the great dragon, he realized his attacks were hitting, but the dragon's body was turning white.

Thomas quickly yelled out, "You're not evil, are you, Zerok?"

"What! I am the great black dragon, mortal. I am the most evil. You must have lost your mind. Now die."

Zerok threw a barrage of black orbs at Thomas, and he stood there to embrace the attack. Hexia had bound Zemarkus, and using her light, she began to burn away one person after another. She realized the more she burned away, the smaller and less powerful Zemarkus became, until they both were on the ground and Zemarkus had devolved into the bartender and a mutated monster clinging to life while vomiting blood.

Hexia, in all her compassion, walked up and placed her hand on his head and said, "It's okay, I forgive you. You may go." With no words, the bartender smiled, turned to ash, and died. At this time, Hexia flew off to aid Thomas only to see him attacked by Zerok. In horror, she yelled out "Nnnnoooooo!" as Thomas took the full force of the attack.

After the smoke cleared, Thomas was unharmed, and the dark bullets turned white. Thomas threw them right back at the dark dragon. The attack destroyed the dark scales of the dragon and revealed white scales.

"I knew it. You couldn't harm me, and you couldn't kill your own sister because you are the true dragon of legend, aren't you? You're the White Dragon of Divinity, Zerok, aren't you?"

With this revelation, Thomas flew up and embraced Zerok's neck, causing light to pour into the dragon. As Zerok screamed in pain, the darkness around him began to dissipate and fade away. Zerok's eyes began to turn from purple to white, and his body became white as snow. As Thomas and Zerok collapsed to the ground with a loud bang, Hexia ran to Thomas to aid him in getting up.

As the two stood up, Zerok opened his gigantic wings and revealed a beautiful white dragon as pure as the snow. Thomas and Hexia bowed to the mighty dragon and said in unison, "Lord Zerok, master of divinity."

Zerok looked at the two and smiled. "My faithful friends, you have freed me from my one thousand years of darkness. I had lived alongside my sister, and together we brought peace to the world. But I became jealous, and through that jealousy grew anger and hatred, and it consumed me. But thanks to you, I have finally been freed. For that, I give you this: to Thomas, I grant the power of immortality, and to Hexia, I grant guardian armor and the Blade of Divinity. With these, I will leave you and restore the kingdom. It is the least I can do."

With that, Zerok turned into a white orb, blasted into the air, and scattered into nothing.

With no words, Thomas and Hexia returned to the village to find everyone restored and healthy, but Gerum was no longer there. As the two held hands, the villagers announced, "Huzzah! Let's praise our new king and queen."

That evening, a ceremony was held for the happy couple to make their coronation and marriage complete. As Thomas looked into Hexia's beautiful eyes, the priest said, "King Thomas, you may kiss the bride."

With that, Thomas leaned in and gave Hexia a great kiss, and the villagers cheered in happiness. The celebration lasted for one week of eating and drinking, and at the end of the festival, Thomas and Hexia returned to their castle to rule the land in peace and prosperity for all time.

The End

ABOUT THE AUTHOR

BRANDON FARLOW WAS born in High Point, North Carolina, and went to school at East Davidson High School. After graduating high school, he joined the United States Army, where he deployed on two tours and spent six years of his life. After returning home for good, he spent the next few years going to college to pursue his passion through graphic design and computer programming, all the while discovering a strong interest in writing. It was during his time in school he reconnected with his high school sweetheart and her eight-year-old son, and the two gradually fell back in love. After two years of being together, his fiancée blessed him with a baby boy, and Brandon and Miranda were married soon after. They finally settled down in a home in Eden, North Carolina, where Brandon continues to pursue his passion for writing, only now he has a loving and supporting family by his side.